**Long-Lost Rossi Siblings**

*Hearts entwine among the vines...*

The Rossis have owned their billion-dollar Tuscan vineyard for centuries. But since tragedy befell the family, Amara and her grandfather have been left to run the Rossi Estate alone. Until they discover the existence of twins, Lorenzo and Daisy—Amara's long-lost half-siblings!

The legacy buried in the estate's soil binds them. Yet, as their family secrets are uncorked, the Rossi siblings find themselves going in three different directions. Each of them unknowingly heading straight towards their perfect pairing... But, after childhoods marred by loss and mistreatment, opening their hearts isn't easy. Love is the most intoxicating vintage—will they be brave enough to take a sip? Find out in...

Amara and Gio's story...
*The Bride Wore His Convenient Ring*
Available now!

And look out for Lorenzo's and Daisy's stories, both coming soon!

Dear Reader,

When I started this book, I wanted a snowy setting with swirls of snowflakes, romantic castles, fairy-tale chalets, roaring fires and lots of lovely food! But most of all, I wanted to tell Amara and Gio's story, a story of two people brought together by fate who truly believe love is not for them. They believe they can forge a marriage contract and keep to its terms. As the story unfolds, they learn that fate has different ideas, and that love isn't something you can negotiate away.

I hope you enjoy reading their story.

*Nina* x

# THE BRIDE WORE HIS CONVENIENT RING

NINA MILNE

ROMANCE

Recycling programs for this product may not exist in your area.

ISBN-13: 978-1-335-47074-4

The Bride Wore His Convenient Ring



For questions and comments about the quality of this book, please contact us at CustomerService@Harlequin.com.

Harlequin Enterprises ULC
22 Adelaide St. West, 41st Floor
Toronto, Ontario M5H 4E3, Canada
www.Harlequin.com

HarperCollins Publishers
Macken House, 39/40 Mayor Street Upper,
Dublin 1, D01 C9W8, Ireland
www.HarperCollins.com

**Printed in U.S.A.**

**Nina Milne** has always dreamed of writing for Harlequin Romance—ever since she played libraries with her mother's stacks of Harlequin romances as a child. On her way to this dream, Nina acquired an English degree, a hero of her own, three gorgeous children and—somehow!—an accountancy qualification. She lives in Brighton and has filled her house with stacks of books—her very own *real* library.

**Books by Nina Milne**

**Harlequin Romance**

***Princesses of Palosia***

*Secret Royal's Napoli Reunion*

***Royal Sarala Weddings***

*His Princess on Paper*
*Bound by Their Royal Baby*

***Summer Escapes***

*Their Mauritius Wedding Ruse*

***The Christmas Pact***

*Snowbound Reunion in Japan*

***Winter Escapes***

*Cinderella's Moroccan Midnight Kiss*

*Consequence of Their Dubai Night*
*Wedding Planner's Deal with the CEO*

Visit the Author Profile page at Harlequin.com for more titles.

To my Mum
for her courage and her positive outlook on life

# PROLOGUE

AMARA ROSSI HAD no idea that her world was about to upend as she walked towards the crenelated, turreted castle with its rugged stone walls, set in the rolling Tuscan hills. Castle Alavario, surrounded by the glorious Rossi vineyards, was the place she had called home for all her twenty-seven years, a place where the Rossi family had lived for centuries.

The word *family* panged pain through her as it always did, the linger of a bone-deep grief. A sense of loss that she'd learnt to live with thanks to her grandfather, Vittorio Rossi, the man who had essentially brought her up. He had been her rock, supported and loved her, been there. In addition, he had imbued her with a sense of her heritage, ensured she'd grown up with a love of the Rossi estate, the vast tumbling sweep of the vineyards, the smell of the grapes at harvest, rich and redolent on the Tuscan air. All of it was a part of her. As the Rossi heir she was determined to ensure that Rossi wines went from strength to strength. The idea that one day it would all be down to her never daunted her, perhaps because it wasn't possible for her to envisage a world without Vittorio in it. The idea one she refused to contemplate, even though she knew no better how foolish that was.

Her steps imperceptibly quickened with a need to see him, to be reassured by his presence, at their daily catch-up in his study.

Minutes later she pushed the heavy arched door open and smiled as her grandfather rose to his feet from behind his leather-topped desk, moved towards her for the customary embrace. As always, he was dressed in a pale crisp shirt, discreetly branded and tucked into a pair of light grey checked trousers with a slim belt demarcating the two; the whole epitomising the fact that Vittorio Rossi was still in his prime, despite the fact he was approaching eighty. That fact backed up by the still thick iron-grey hair and the brightness of the chocolate-brown eyes that characterised the Rossi family.

An eye colour that Amara didn't share; she had inherited her mother's green eyes and a mane of red hair to go with it.

'I've opened a bottle of our favourite Chianti,' he said. 'I thought tonight we could talk over a glass before we eat.'

Amara stepped back and studied her grandfather's face, caught a touch of reserve in his voice, saw something in the brown eyes. A suppressed excitement alongside a touch of anxiety.

'That sounds good,' she said carefully. 'What's the occasion?'

'I have some news,' Vittorio said.

A sudden sense of foreboding trickled through Amara even as she told herself not to catastrophise. It could be good news after all. Whatever it was she knew it must be significant to warrant a bottle from one of their best years, the wine made from her favourite Sangiovese grape. She accepted the carefully poured glass with a smile of thanks and for a precious second they both sipped the deep ruby red liquid, savoured the intense taste of ripe red berries that lingered on the palate. Both of them recalling the harvest from a year that had produced such a good crop.

Then Vittorio walked towards the fireplace, placed his glass on the mantelpiece and turned.

'I am not sure of the best way to put this Amara. So, I'll just say it. It turns out that you have a half-brother and half-sister.' He hesitated. 'Twins.'

The world seemed to spin and for a second, she thought the heavy crystal glass was about to drop from her hand. Summoning every ounce of control, she forced herself to remain completely still, then she instructed her feet to move, one step at a time towards the polished teak sideboard where she oh, so carefully placed the glass down.

'I don't understand,' she said, amazed that her voice could sound so calm, her brain telling her that this wasn't possible, it didn't make sense. That this was all some sort of hallucination, a dream, a joke.

'It was a shock to me as well,' Vittorio said. 'A few weeks ago, I received a letter from a Lorenzo Cavendish. He said he had found documentation that suggested we could be related. It was plausible enough that I agreed to DNA testing. It is the truth Amara. Lorenzo and you are siblings.'

'But…how? When?' It didn't make sense, couldn't make sense.

'Lorenzo and Daisy are two years older than you. They have grown up not knowing their true father.'

'But…did my father know about them?'

Amara's brain was spinning now, and with each spin it felt as though her carefully constructed world was shattering. Ever since the accident it had been her and her grandfather, a safe dependable unit, a format she had based her life on. And her memories of her parents, or at least the idea she had constructed, had been based on a devoted couple, childhood sweethearts. Now her brain started to do the math. Her parents had been married for three years before she had been born. That meant her father had been unfaithful. Now hysteria threatened—she had twin siblings. The irony pierced her soul, poked at the jagged wound left from the loss of her own twin brother, who had perished along with her parents in the tragic helicopter accident that had changed the course of her life, and ended Luca's just days after their fourth birthday.

'Yes. It appears that Roberto did know about the pregnancy.' Vittorio's voice was sad now and instinctively Amara put her own thoughts aside, realised what a shock this must have been for her grandfather. 'But he made a decision to walk away. It looks as though he cut off all contact with Lorenzo and Daisy's mother when she told him she was pregnant.' Vittorio raised his hands. 'I know this is hard Amara but I think we should focus on the positive.'

'What positives?'

Right now, she couldn't see any, didn't want to believe that her father had behaved so dishonourably, certainly had no wish to have new siblings. She'd lost her twin. It was a loss that she knew would sear her forever; she didn't want a replacement brother or a sister. She certainly didn't want both. For an instant she tried to picture it, tried to imagine a brother and a sister sitting in this very study. Everyone smiling, laughing, discussing the year's harvest. The type of family scene that she had pictured so many times with a sense of yearning and what might have beens. Only in her imagination it had been herself and Luca sat on the leather armchairs, her parents stood with Vittorio at the mantelpiece. An alternative timeline where the accident hadn't happened, where she had grown up with a family.

But it wasn't like that. For twenty-three years it had been herself and Vittorio and that was how she liked it. The idea of a new, larger family made panic rise and swirl inside her. She and Vittorio were a unit that she understood, relied on, felt secure with. Another thought crept in, she was the Rossi heir, she loved every vine, every acre, every furrow of Rossi land. It was her inheritance. She shook her head, knew that at least was unworthy. Lorenzo and Daisy hadn't had a chance to know about the estate, had been robbed of that chance by her father. *Their* father. The thought sent a tremor of rejection through her, the idea repugnant, unacceptable. Impossible.

No. It was possible. More than that, it was fact.

Vittorio Rossi was nobody's fool; he would not be telling her this unless it was truth.

'They are family,' Vittorio said. 'Rossi blood runs through their veins. They could be a *good* addition to our lives. I am getting older. And as I do one of my biggest worries is leaving you alone.'

Hearing the emotion in her grandfather's voice, she pushed her own feelings to one side, as she moved towards him. 'It is all right, Nonno. You will be around for a lot longer yet and you need not be concerned for me. You have taught me so much that there is no need for you to worry about what will happen in the future. I swear to you that I will look after the Rossi estate, it will continue to thrive and flourish. I love this land—it is in my blood.'

'I know that, Amara. But…' Her grandfather

hesitated. 'I trust you. But it may feel…lonely. And what about after that? Future generations? I would never pressure you into a marriage or ask that you have children simply to provide an heir but…'

But—that one syllable somehow said so much and further emotions piled in as her grandfather skirted a topic they had always studiously avoided ever since Amara's first relationship had fizzled out. Then her second. Amara had tried, she really had. But she couldn't do it, could not navigate a relationship. It was as though there was a switch inside her that was permanently switched to off. Her two brief forays had not been successful; letting anyone in was too hard, made her too uncomfortable, too panicked.

Not for the first time she wondered where that left her. She knew love was not for her, not when she knew how easily it could be lost in a blink of an eye, how fragile the threads that bound people were. Tragedy could strike completely unannounced, or events that were out of your control could tornado in and destroy what had been built up. Better to walk alone, to make sure you and only you were in control of as much as it was possible to control.

Which meant of course there was a question mark over the future. The Rossi vineyards had been tended by Rossis for centuries; what would happen after Amara?

'Do they, Lorenzo and Daisy, have children?' she asked, a sudden sense of displacement hitting her; so strong that she realised she was clenching her hand around the back of a brocaded chair, the beaded material cutting into her fingers.

'Not that I am aware.'

But they might, or they might be in happy relationships. Perhaps her newly found siblings understood how to navigate all the pitfalls and minefields that relationships seemed to bring. Rendering the whole shebang pointless. Why engage in something perilous, in something that could bring hurt and pain and profound loss in a blink of an eye? Looking at Vittorio now, though, she knew the answer. A relationship would bring children, heirs to continue the Rossi dynasty. How could her grandfather not welcome that possibility?

'This is very early days,' Vittorio continued. 'I know very little about them, except that Lorenzo is a very successful businessman in his own right. But I would like to invite them to come to visit the estate, to meet us. Roberto was my son and I loved him, but what he did was wrong. Lorenzo and Daisy are his children and they were his responsibility. They are Rossis even if they bear a different name. I believe we have a moral duty to welcome them. But also would it be so bad to have a larger family circle? We lost so much. These people—they are family.'

Amara gathered herself together; she would not hurt this man, a man she loved with all her heart. This was important to him and how could she blame him for that? Tragedy had taken so much from him, his wife as well as his son, daughter-in-law and grandson. He'd then had the responsibility of bringing up a four-year-old on his own. This was his chance to have more family, a chance to make the future of the Rossi heritage safer. She had to respect that—she owed him that and so much more.

Moving across to him she gave him a hug. 'I understand. Of course, I do. And of course, I will welcome them. But...' Not yet. She needed time to get her head round the sheer enormity of what had happened. 'It has been a lot to take in. I think I need a little time to reflect. To think.' To work out a strategy that would enable her to put a good face on this, even as she felt an inner determination to hold these newcomers at bay. They may be predators; whatever they were they could not replace her real family.

'Of course you do.' Her grandfather's voice full of understanding. 'Why don't you go away for a week? Have a break. A holiday. I will contact Lorenzo and see what his feelings are about a meet up.'

# CHAPTER ONE

GIOVANNI ROMANO ENTERED the busy hotel restaurant with an impatient stride. A day on the ski slopes, nestled in the grandeur of the Bavarian Alps, should have improved his mood. But the adrenalin from his curving, swooping descents had done nothing to satisfactorily distract him from his thoughts. His subsequent stint in the pool, lap after rhythmic lap followed by the heat of a sauna, hadn't bolstered his thought process or brought him any closer to a conclusion as to what to do.

No closer to an answer to a life-changing decision. Did he want to become part of a family firm when his family, with the exception of his grandparents, couldn't stand him? If he did want to, how would he fulfil the conditions that were part of the deal?

He didn't need to do this; he was a multimillionaire in his own right, had his own company to run. More pertinently, he'd spent his entire childhood with one clear ambition—to sever his family ties and live his own life unfettered by family bonds. Any bonds.

But now his grandparents had asked for his help. Asked him to enter the Romano business empire. A supreme irony, seeing that Gio had been excluded from the family company from his birth. He had been given the Romano name but nothing that went with it except a childhood where he'd spent months of every year in forced proximity with his father, stepmother and two half-brothers, a proximity rendered horrific by their treatment of him. Inclusion in the echelons of Romano Confectionery—that was for real family. Whilst Gio was simply a second-class Romano, evidence of a deeply regretted, extremely brief marriage between his father, Salvatore Romano, and his mother, wild child, rock star Luna Rocca.

But all that had changed now. Now his grandparents *wanted* to bring Gio in. The idea still seemed fantastical, filled him with disbelief and elation that he, Gio Romano, could be admitted, invited to the hallowed boardroom of Romano Confectionery.

Gio ran through the facts in his head. Or at least the facts his grandparents had shared. Unease nudged him; he had the feeling they had been holding something back, but he didn't know what.

Fact: now in their eighties Aurelio and Ava Romano had decided to step back from the company. Fact: they had handed over some of their shares to Salvatore. Fact: unsurprisingly, in Gio's opinion, now they regretted that decision because Salvatore was doing things his way, according to *his* vision. A vision that did not accord with his grandparents'. Or with Gio's come to that.

Gio knew exactly how low his father would go, believed implicitly that Salvatore would have no qualms in inflicting a cost-cutting regime, would sacrifice quality for profit and in so doing would ruin Romano Confectionery's reputation for high standards, would undermine the ethos the company had been built on. And in so doing he could well ruin it. Breaking Aurelio and Ava Romano's hearts. Gio couldn't let that happen.

But…next fact: he still didn't really understand why his grandparents needed Gio, they still retained enough shares to outvote Salvatore.

Instead they wanted to bring Gio in, give him a controlling number of shares and appoint him to the board as a 'counterbalance'.

They *said* the company needed new blood, *said* they didn't want the scandal and bad publicity associated with sacking their son, *said* that it would be difficult given the number of shares he owned and the fact he had the support of the rest of the board.'

It made a certain sense, but Gio couldn't help feeling he was still being manoeuvred, was still a Romano pawn, being moved across the Romano chess board.

Which brought on the next problem. Because the articles of Romano Confectionery, written by its founders Max and Elisabetta Romano stipulated that family board members had to be married. His great-grandparents had had a clear vision for the company's future, which stated that, 'we want this to be a family business that continues for generations. Therefore, we stipulate that any family member admitted to the board must be married. This will ensure a commitment to producing a future generation and also ensure they have a settled, responsible lifestyle allowing them to fully commit to the business.'

So Gio would need to get married, a state he had avoided for years. Commitment was not for him. He believed in keeping a distance because that way you didn't get sucked in, you retained control of your own life.

Yet he was considering it because he owed his grandparents, cared about them; their relationship a complex one, that even now Gio didn't fully understand. But he did know that his grandparents had intervened to end the bullying, the humiliations inflicted on him by his father, his stepmother and his brothers. Had made his childhood more bearable. Once they had discovered the bullying, they had even taken an interest in his life and over the years he had become close to them. Or as close as it was possible for him to be with anyone. He didn't believe Aurelio and Ava loved him, but they at least had the decency, the morality, to take some responsibility for him, which was more than either of his parents had done.

His mind still whirring, his eyes scanned the restaurant. The spacious room was full of diners, tables arranged to maximise table space but yet ensure privacy. The décor combined a sense of splendour with a surprising intimacy, the walls a deep red, the dark wooden tables lit by artfully placed wall and overhead copper-coloured lights and separated by impressive pillars and swathes of russet and shimmering gold fabrics.

There were couples who'd headed to the Bavarian Alps for a post-Christmas winter vacation, interspersed with larger groups of business convention delegates gathered to discuss the new year ahead. His eye fell on the only table set for one. His table, he assumed, as a staff member walked up.

'Good evening, Matteo.' The same waiter from the previous night who he'd engaged in conversation.

'Mr Romano. Come this way.' Gio followed him to the table, sat down and picked up the menu.

'I'll be back in a few minutes,' Matteo said. But in fact, Gio had barely glanced at the menu before Matteo returned, a slightly worried look on his face, accompanied by a woman.

Gio blinked; the woman had a glorious cascade of red hair that shimmered with tones of auburn, russet and a glimmer of copper and fell in waves to below her shoulders, framing a delicate face with luminous green eyes, a straight nose and glossy lips that he had to force himself not to focus on. Dressed in an elegant grey cashmere dress, made slightly different by a knotted side that emphasised her slender waist before falling into a skirt that fell to mid-calf, she took his breath away. He knew he should stop staring, but he was captivated and as his eyes met hers, he saw a spark in the emerald hue, an answering arrest as if she too were caught in the sudden iridescent mesh of attraction. *Whoa.* Enough. Now was not the time to become enmeshed in any sort of attraction, mutual or not. At the exact same instant, they both broke eye contact.

Matteo turned to the woman. 'I am so sorry. I really can't apologise enough. There has been a mix-up. Both of you ordered a table for one and somehow...'

'We've both been given the same table?' the woman enquired; her tone neutral rather than censorious.

'Exactly.'

She looked round the crowded room. 'It's okay. Mistakes happen. Perhaps I could be given a different table.'

Matteo now looked harried. 'I am not sure... we are very busy today. There is a concert being held later and I don't believe there will be a table free for a couple more hours. I could try but...' His voice trailed off.

'Or,' Gio heard his voice say. 'I am happy to share the table.' Told himself it was common sense, common courtesy. Nothing more.

The waiter looked hopeful. 'If that would

suit, of course that would be no problem for us, Mr Romano.'

The woman hesitated, glanced around the crowded dining room as if searching for a different table, any table, then back at Gio and he could see a reluctance that he'd swear was personal. Then the expression passed, her green eyes took in Matteo's worried, hopeful expression and her lips turned upwards in a polite smile with a hint of rue.

'Thank you for the offer, Mr Romano. If you're sure it's not a problem, I accept.'

'No problem at all,' Gio said aware of a misplaced sense of anticipation as she sat down opposite him and smiled her thanks as Matteo set her place and then left them with a promise to return for their order.

He watched as she studied the menu, noted the expression of concentration as she read it. As if sensing his gaze she looked up. 'Sorry. I take my food seriously. This may take some time.'

'That's fine with me.' Gio took the chance to study her face properly, in an attempt to work out what it was about her that was continuing to poleaxe him. He watched as she turned her attention to the wine menu and then glanced back up at him and he hurriedly perused his menu, just as Matteo returned.

Gio waited as she ordered and then Matteo turned to him. 'And for you?'

'I'll have…' he stared at the menu and then back up. 'Actually, that sounds so good I'll have the same.'

Once Matteo had gone, Gio looked across at his dinner companion. 'I'm sorry about the mix-up with the table, especially as I get the feeling you'd rather have had dinner alone.'

'It's not your fault,' she said. 'I was planning on eating alone with a book for company, so I didn't want to share a table with anyone, and esp—' she broke off, consternation on her face.

'Especially not me?' he finished for her.

'I'm sorry. I didn't mean to say that. I'm just not used to having dinner with someone like you, with your reputation.'

Her voice was even and he sensed the apology was sincere, but the words still caught him on the raw, even as he told himself there was no need for him to explain or justify his reputation. That was the beauty of his life—he answered to no one, could live his life as he wished. Had no dependants, was responsible for no one's happiness. That allowed him to live the lifestyle he lived, one where he worked hard and partied hard.

Just like his mother did but with a crucial difference. Gio had a clear remit to hurt no one. Luna hadn't cared who got hurt in the process, not the various men she pursued and discarded and not her son either. Luna Rocco had never let the minor matter of parenthood cramp her style at all.

She'd never been actively unkind to him; she was even carelessly fond of him, but it would never have occurred to her to curtail her excesses or change the way she lived or put herself out in the slightest for her son. At any age or time. Gio had grown up cast into the care of various staff members of Luna Rocco's entourage, many of whom definitely had no child care qualifications. Interspersed with this had been the even worse sojourns with his father. So, his whole childhood he'd looked forward to the day he would be in control of his own life, no longer reliant on the whims of others. And that's where he was now, so he had no intention of explaining anything to this woman. That he was not like his mother, someone who pursued what she wanted without much, if any, thought for the impact it had on others.

That was his business. So maybe he should

call this now, suggest he leave this woman to the solitary meal she clearly wanted and was entitled to.

But before he could speak, he realised she was studying his face, her expression intent and then to his surprise she gave a small rueful smile and raised a hand, contrition in her green eyes and in her voice. ‘I shouldn’t have said that. I’m really sorry. I don’t know you and I shouldn’t judge you on a few articles I read in my dentist’s waiting room. Can we start again?’

There was a silence as brown eyes met green.

Amara took a deep breath, held his gaze as she waited for his answer, wondered why she’d even asked the question. Wondered what the hell was going on. Ever since she’d set eyes on Giovanni Romano something had happened to her. A sudden, instant, ridiculous reaction to him. One look and she’d been bowled over, her body on high alert, a funny dipping sensation in her stomach and she didn’t like it. Liked it even less when she’d realised his identity.

Because it was galling to admit that she’d succumbed to his charms just like the string of women he’d dated, according to the articles she’d read. They identified Gio Romano, son of rock star Luna Rocco, as a Lothario who went through women at speed. A man with a reputation for being a serial dater of celebrities.

A few days ago, his reputation probably wouldn't have resonated with her so much. But tonight, it did. Who knew how many women he'd hurt, or betrayed. Like her father had betrayed her mother. Had her father loved Lorenzo and Daisy's mother? Or just slept with her? Once, numerous times… Come to that, for all she knew her father had had a string of affaires. The only reason she knew about this one was there had been a consequence. Two babies.

The idea, the knowledge, had shattered her world. So right now, Amara had no tolerance for men who played the field. Men like the man she was now sat opposite. The man who her errant body had identified as the bee's knees.

But then she'd seen his expression, seen something she'd swear was anger and hurt touch his brown eyes, and she'd known that she'd struck a nerve and had a sudden strong, albeit irrational, sense that she was somehow in the wrong. A feeling that grew as their gazes locked, the moment stretching.

Without thinking, she reached out and touched his hand, and as she did so something fizzed through her, the jolt of awareness, the sense of connection so intense she snatched her hand back and just stared at his. Focused on its shape, its strength, and imagined the imprint of his fingers on her.

Her gaze jerked up and she met his eyes, saw a mirrored shock in their brown depths, and a flash of desire so strong she felt her body heat up in response.

She had to get a grip; she must have imagined her reaction. She must have.

Gio blinked, gave his head a small shake, and she'd swear his brain was scrambling to recall the question she'd asked. Then he visibly pulled himself together.

'Yes,' he said. 'Let's start again.' He held his hand out. 'Hi. I am Gio Romano and you are?'

Amara glanced down at his hand and then back at him, was met with a wide-eyed look of innocence with a hint of a challenge. Fine. Maybe he wanted to test whether or not that earlier reaction was a blip. Well, so did she, to prove that whatever had happened earlier was some sort of strange one-off reaction. Not to be repeated.

Yet as she continued to look at the outstretched hand, once again she could feel something bubble up inside her, and in an almost abrupt movement she grasped his hand and bit back an expletive.

Holy moly. She had no idea what was going on but the earlier reaction had not been an isolated one. The feel of his hand round hers was causing her pulse rate to pound and was certainly enough for her to tell herself she had to make sure there were absolutely no more touches, even as she realised her hand still rested in his, his grasp firm and welcome and…

Right now, she couldn't even remember why she was holding his hand; all she knew was she didn't want to let go.

The sound of a throat clearing brought her to her senses and she dropped his hand, looked up at Matteo's carefully expressionless face.

'Your food,' he said.

Amara realised for once in her life she had no idea what she'd even ordered, studied the plate Matteo carefully placed in front of her, her brain scrambling to even identify its contents. Her only consolation that Gio looked as shell-shocked as she did.

'This looks… incredible,' she finally managed.

'And smells as good as it looks,' Gio said and credit to him that he sounded so together. 'My compliments to the chef and all the kitchen staff.'

Once Matteo had gone, Amara focused on the smells that wafted up from her plate, on the light colour of the Grüner Veltliner she'd ordered to go with the food. This was what she knew, what she understood. Tastes, flavours, blends, smells, scents, wine…this was her forte, her world, a place where she was confident. A place where physical desire, the force of attraction had no place, a lexicon outside her comprehension. It was important not to give this attraction any power; just because it existed there was no need to overreact to it. One dinner and they'd go their separate ways.

A deep breath and she looked across at him.

'I still don't even know your name,' he said.

'Um, right. Sorry. I'm Amara. Amara Rossi. Pleased to meet you.' Possibly.

# CHAPTER TWO

GIO WONDERED WHAT the hell was going on. If shaking hands could cause that level of reaction what would happen if he kissed her? He closed his eyes. He was *not* going to kiss her. For a start this was not a date. He was in the Bavarian Alps to consider his future; come to that, if he agreed to his grandparents' proposal, soon enough he'd be getting married. Possibly to one of the suitable women his grandparents apparently had lined up for him. Again, the sensation of being expertly guided across a board crossed his mind.

'I am pleased to meet you, too,' he said. 'And please note that if at any point you would prefer to read your book please go ahead.'

She shook her head. 'Thanks, but I'm good. It wouldn't feel right when this food deserves all my attention.' She sighed. 'Anyway, I'm not sure it would work. I love the author, but somehow, for once, reading isn't really working as a distraction. I read the same page ten times on the plane and it didn't go in.'

The idea that she was looking for a distraction triggered a strange sense of connection, highlighted the feeling of warmth that she had revised her original opinion of him, that she had genuinely seemed to get his philosophy.

'Tell me about it.' He gestured to his laptop. 'I was planning on a working dinner. Because earlier I read the same page of a report ten times and I can't remember a word of it. And seeing that I wrote it, that's a bit worrying.'

'If you would rather work that's fine.'

He shook his head. 'I think I'd far rather be distracted by you.'

Amara looked as though she wasn't quite sure how to take that and settled for, 'Well let's hope we both manage to enjoy the food. It looks incredible.'

'It does,' he said. 'Even though I have to admit I'm not sure what it actually is. I was already a bit distracted when we ordered.'

'By what?' she asked, her eyes narrowed in suspicion.

'You,' he said simply and truthfully, as a sense of recklessness emerged. Of course, he wasn't going to act on attraction, but surely a little bit of banter was allowable. It sounded as though it could be a welcome distraction for them both.

'Oh.' She looked down and then back up at him, as if she too had made a decision, putting her hand up in mock defence. 'Is this some of the famed Romano charm?' Now her lips upturned into a delightfully impish smile.

'Absolutely not. That was the unvarnished truth. The Romano charm only comes into play on a date. This is a chance meeting.' The words, though said lightly, seemed to resonate, and for some reason a little tingle ran over his skin. As if he was being touched by the hand of fate. He blinked the fanciful thought away.

'So, what comes into play on chance encounters?'

'I have no idea. I'm making this up as we go. Feel free to say what *you* want from this.'

There was a silence, and as their eyes met there it was again, the zip and zing, the pull and push of attraction.

'Nothing complicated,' she said softly and there was a husk to her voice. 'A simple, friendly dinner.'

'Hmm. How friendly would you like to be?' he asked, exaggerating his tone into a drawl, adding an eyebrow wiggle for extra effect.

Her green eyes widened and then she

laughed, a genuine ring of laughter and a disproportionate sense of satisfaction warmed him.

'Friendly enough to enjoy the food and the company,' she said. 'In that order,' she added. 'This is delicious. And so you know, we're having truffle tagliolini with a Prosecco foam to start with. Followed by sea bass cooked with a special caper sauce and lemon and chard with fondant potatoes.'

'Simple but not the sort of thing you'd usually have at home,' he said.

'Exactly. Though it is Italian, so maybe I am feeling a little homesick. But definitely not your normal fare. Did you know that truffles grow underground as compared to mushrooms that grow overground, and there are truffle hunters who use trained dogs to find the truffles?'

He gave a sudden smile. 'I didn't know that.'

'I am a mine of trivial food information,' she said lightly. 'And I have always wanted to try Prosecco foam, though I have to admit I have no idea how to make it.'

She tipped her head to one side, as she took a small first mouthful and he could see her actually savour the taste and flavours. 'Mmm. The pasta really works—it's like spaghetti but flatter so the texture is great. And the truffle is amazing.'

Gio took a bite and nodded. She was right, though right now he was more focused on watching Amara, seeing the focus, the concentration on her face, the way her forehead creased slightly, the slight jut to her chin.

'Kind of nutty, oaky. It reminds me of woods or forests.' She broke off. 'It's a good thing this *isn't* a date.'

'Why's that?'

'Because I can focus on eating and savouring every mouthful. My ex used to get annoyed because I took so long to eat and drink. Plus the running commentary.'

'Feel free to take your time. Personally, I'm in agreement with you. Food is far too important to rush. I believe in taking my time over pleasurable things.'

One part of his mind wondered what the hell he was doing. The other didn't care, revelled in the tinge of colour that touched her cheeks, even as he wondered if he'd gone too far. He didn't want to spook her or actually make her uncomfortable. But as he was about to apologise, she smiled right back.

'That's always good to know,' she said, each word slow and drawn out, her voice low. Her eyes met his and he could see his own desire mirrored in the green depths of her eyes. A desire that was swiftly superseded by shock and she blinked rapidly, picked up her wine glass and sipped carefully. He could almost see her ground herself. 'It's important to appreciate good food and wine,' she said, her voice commendably even.

'Yes.' Hell, was that strangled voice really his? He couldn't take his eyes off her, and dammit, he wasn't thinking about the pleasure of food or wine and he was sure that neither was she.

But she was at least trying to steer the conversation to smoother, safer waters. The least he could do was attempt the same. Think. Conversation.

'What brings you to the Bavarian Alps? Are you here on pleasure…' Really Gio? 'Or business?' It was abrupt, but it truly was all he could think of. Other than kissing her. Tasting the wine via her lips.

Her gaze skimmed his lips and he knew she was struggling as much as he was. 'Um… It's a few days' break,' she said. 'Though I may try and include some business and make a trip to a winery over here. My grandfather owns a vineyard in Tuscany. I live and work there.'

'That sounds fascinating,' he said. 'It must be incredible watching it all from start to finish.'

'It is. I've been living, breathing and drinking wine since I was born.' There was an emphasis in her voice he couldn't quite identify. 'I can't imagine working anywhere else. And whilst obviously I think Italian wine, or at least our Italian wine, is the best in the world, I am open to learning from and enjoying produce from other countries. So, I'd be interested to visit a Bavarian winery.'

'Even though you're on holiday?'

'It's not exactly a holiday. I came here…to… think,' she said quietly. 'I thought a change of scene and solitude would help. Usually walking round the estate works, but this time it seemed important to be away.' She shook her head as if regretting the words. 'What about you?'

'Oddly enough I am here for the same reasons you are. I wanted to clear my head and think. I'm at a cross-road in my life. I have a choice I need to make and for the first time in a long time I am conflicted. I can't make a decision and that's a novelty for me.'

He'd mapped out his path in life from the moment he'd realised the importance of being in control. As a child he'd been at the mercy of his parents' whims, shunted from chaos at his mother's to misery at his father's. All he'd wanted to do was be in charge of his own life. To live it on his own terms.

Amara sipped her wine, smiled up at Matteo as he brought their next course, waited until he'd placed their plates in front of them. 'At least you are in control of your decision. It's something you *can* make a choice about. You are in charge of your own destiny.'

'Aren't you in control of yours?'

'It doesn't feel like that right now. But then again, I'm not sure anyone is in complete control of their own destiny. Fate has a habit of intruding.'

Like today, he wondered. 'Sure. But you can still call the shots to a degree. Some decisions are just harder than others to make.'

'I know.' She sighed. 'Right now, for me it's not so much about making a choice. It's more about coming to terms. Acceptance. But the more I think about it the more I'm struggling.'

'I get that. The more I think the more I can't decide.'

She gestured to the tables around them. 'Maybe that's the point of commitment. All these couples. When there's a decision to be made you've at least got someone to talk it over with.'

'But then you've also got their welfare to think about. And you may disagree, which makes it all even harder. At least I'm only arguing with myself.' He couldn't miss the opportunity. 'Then you're not married. Or in a relationship?'

'Absolutely not.' She sounded as though the concept was a difficult one to grasp, but there was a hint of sadness there too. 'I'm not interested in any length of commitment.'

A shadow crossed her eyes and he could see too that her face held signs of tiredness, sensed that whatever situation she was facing it matched his own. Curiosity was superseded by something else—a desire to help, to smooth away the strain.

'So, your plan for the next few days is to think over your situation on your own? Whilst reading your book as a distraction.'

She nodded. 'That about sums it up.'

'Then I've got an idea.' The words seemed to be stringing together almost without his brain's involvement. 'I am planning to go on a hike tomorrow. See if the beauty of the Alps, the fresh air, the snow underfoot will help me get some perspective. Would you like to join me? Maybe company will work better than a book or a work report as a distraction.'

There was a silence and then to his surprise and perhaps her own she gave a small mischievous smile. 'You're asking me to come along to distract you?'

Gio gulped. Her smile, which made her green eyes sparkle and this time revealed an enchanting dimple in her right cheek that completely captivated him, took his breath away.

'Yup. But I'll return the favour. It'll be a mutual distraction pact. What do you think?'

There was a pause and her smile widened. 'Sounds like a plan.'

The next morning Amara opened her eyes, looked around the unfamiliar room as memories of where she was filtered in. Leaning back on the luxurious pillows she took in the terracotta and cream décor, the clean lines of the room, with its gleaming wooden floor and light-coloured furniture. The neutral colours enlivened and brightened by the luxurious handmade wool rugs, a hue of red she'd never seen before and the thick brocade of the russet curtains, behind which she knew were nearly floor-to-ceiling windows that provided a glorious panoramic view of snow-dusted terrain. Blinking away the aftermath of her dreams, she was aware of a bubble of anticipation that had lightened the sense of weightiness that she'd carried since that conversation with her grandfather. A bubble that expanded as she got ready, aware that she was taking extra care as she brushed her hair, applied a touch of mascara to emphasise her eyes. Stopped there. Gio Romano was a distraction. Nothing more.

That was why she'd agreed to this hike. They were both here because life had thrown them a curveball. The attraction was irrelevant. In fact, maybe it wasn't Gio per se she was attracted to—it was the distraction he provided.

Amara had the feeling there was a flaw in her logic, knew she had to tread warily. Whatever the reason for it, she would not give into this attraction, would not give it power.

Yet it was hard to remember that as, half an hour later, she headed across the opulent hotel lobby. She tried to focus on the sense of space, the parquet floor with its dark red inlays, the wide sweeping pillars, the wall enclosures containing vases and statues from different corners of the globe, delicate blue and white china and fluting Venetian glass. But her eyes kept honing in on Gio, and, as she approached, her heartbeat accelerated as she took in his height, his breadth, the muscular whole. He was dressed for the weather in a dark blue down jacket, his dark brown eyes looking at her with a warmth that sent her heart even faster. He looked… Utterly scrummy. Scrummy? *Really, Amara?* She must be in a bad way—scrummy was not in her usual vocabulary.

Forcing herself to keep her steps even and a polite smile on her face, she approached.

'Good morning,' he said and handed her a steaming cup. 'Hot chocolate. Proper hot chocolate.'

She accepted the cup as they exited the lobby and stepped out into the magnificence of the hotel grounds. Stopping, she turned to look at the sprawl of the building with its hipped pyramid roof, turrets and Art Deco–styled architecture. Took in the utter beauty of the landscape. The building was nestled at the foot of a sloping valley of forests, the trees peeking dark green through layers of snow on one side whilst in the distance majestic jagged ice-peaked mountains loomed and spiked grandly up to the clear cold blue sky.

Turning, she saw Gio indicating a path headed towards a sloping hill. 'I thought we'd go that way,' he suggested. 'It's about an hour's walk to a restaurant which apparently does an amazing fondue.'

'Sounds good to me.'

As they started to walk, the snow crisp and crunchy under their booted feet, she inhaled the aroma of the hot chocolate appreciatively. 'This smells gorgeous,' she said. 'Rich and dark and I can smell cocoa with a hint of vanilla.' She broke off, remembered how much her tendency to analyse everything she ate and drank had annoyed both Stefan and Silvio. Better to continue to walk in silence and take in the beauty of the scenery around her, the scattered snow-coated pine trees that sent a scent of evergreen to mingle with the tang of unshed snow in the air.

But the memory of her failed relationships had triggered a reminder of her own shortcomings, her inability to let anyone close, a failing that was a deep disappointment to her grandfather, the person she loved most in the world, the person she owed everything to.

No wonder Lorenzo and Daisy had given Vittorio hope for the future. A hope for heirs. No wonder her grandfather wanted to welcome them into the family. Of course Amara would be by his side.

Though how long for? Because somehow, she felt displaced; felt outnumbered. She *was* outnumbered by Lorenzo and Daisy; twins who would share the same bond that she and

Luca had once shared. A bond she still felt. So how could she welcome Lorenzo and Daisy? How could she possibly allow herself to get close to new siblings, even if she could figure out how to. Even if she wanted to.

And now she winced as an image flashed in front of her eyes. A memory of running through the vineyards with her twin. They had been so close; in games of hide-and-seek they had always been able to find the other, sensed where the other was hiding.

But Luca was gone now, had barely had a taste of life.

Instead, there were two adults, two newly minted Rossis, a unit. And there was Amara… Alone. And that was how it would stay. How could she betray Luca's memory when the pain of his loss was still so raw? And any sort of real connection to Lorenzo and Daisy *would be* a betrayal, as if it were possible to replace Luca, forget him. It would somehow devalue his memory, dilute it, reduce him. The very idea jarred through her.

'You okay?'

Amara blinked, turned her head to meet Gio's brown eyes.

'You're marching like a woman on a mission and I'm pretty sure I can see steam coming out of your ears. Any second now the snow will melt.'

To her surprise she realised he was right. She slowed down and took a deep breath.

'Sorry. Yes, I am angry.'

'Believe me, I get it.' He gave her a rueful smile and her anger almost started to recede, almost pushed away by the sheer wattage, the way little lines crinkled around his brown eyes, the crease in his cheeks, the set of his jaw, the shape of his mouth. Almost.

'You can't get it,' she said, the anger holding strong and now directed against if not him, then herself, for almost believing him.

'Try me,' he said and paused as the meaning of his words blurred. And suddenly, somehow in that pause anger and frustration morphed into something else, different emotions colliding and bouncing—push and pulling an urge to throw caution to the wind, to try his lips, try to see what kissing him would be like. And the pause stretched.

Their gazes locked and silence reigned; a silence that seemed to blanket the moment, the air cold and crisp, and as if of their own volition her feet took a step towards him and as if in answer, he too closed the gap between them and Amara knew exactly what would help. Damn it, she wanted to take that final step, grab him by his jacket, pull him down and lock her lips against his. The desire so intense, the image so clear, the anticipation so head spinning that for one mad, glorious instant she nearly translated words to action.

What *was* happening to her? This heady sense of anticipation, this churn of desire was so alien to her. But she knew it was to do with Gio Romano's presence, something in the air that was turning her into someone intent on flirting with danger.

Because this was dangerous—it was something she didn't understand, another unexpected twist and she didn't like it. Or perhaps the problem was she did like it, this head-whirling distraction. But surely the fact that he was good-looking, try utterly drop-dead gorgeous, should not be playing riot with her hormones like this.

Shouldn't be turning her insides to mush, her legs to jelly and worse, urging her to take one more step forward. This wasn't what Amara Rossi did. Not her style. This man had a reputation, most likely a merited one, even if she'd decided it was none of her business.

In a movement so abrupt she almost fell over she leapt awkwardly backwards and he reached out a hand to steady her. Amara forced herself not to react, reminded herself that her coat was insulated dammit, so she couldn't possibly be feeling anything. Carefully now, she took another step backwards.

'Try you,' she repeated.

He nodded now, took a deep breath and a step backwards as if he too needed distance. 'I think I do get it. From what you said yesterday, I think you have found yourself in a situation you feel you can't control, a situation that has come about through no fault or action of your own. Yet it impacts you and that is making you feel mad because you have limited options and you don't like any of them. That would make me feel pretty mad too, because it makes you feel like a chess piece being moved across the board at the whim of someone else, playing a strategy where you count for nothing.'

Amara stared at him and realised virtual stranger or not, playboy or not, he did get it; knew that his insight could only come from empathy. 'You do get it.'

He gave a small smile, one that invited trust. 'If you want to talk to me, tell me more, maybe I can help. Or maybe just sharing will help.'

Amara studied Gio's expression, saw seriousness there and sincerity. Could she trust the instinct telling her that, or was that instinct coloured by the tug of attraction, his sheer proximity?

Did it matter? Gio was a stranger, a man she'd never see again; in some ways maybe he was the perfect person to confide in. Perhaps he could help see through the tangle of her thoughts, have a clarity of perspective.

# CHAPTER THREE

GIO WATCHED AMARA as she considered his offer, an offer he had meant. He did want to help. With an intensity he didn't quite understand, any more than he understood the sense of connection. But he wanted to do something to push back the shadows under her eyes, the strain of tiredness, the trudge of her feet in the snow before they'd progressed to a stamp.

He watched as she came to a decision. 'Perhaps it will,' she said. She paused for a moment as if marshalling her thoughts 'I told you that I was brought up on the Rossi estate. The estate has belonged to the Rossi family since the twelfth century, and we've been producing wine for hundreds of years. We aren't the largest estate in Italy or the best-known but we are successful and I am proud of the wine we produce.' He could hear that pride in her voice, wondered what that must feel like, to be an accepted member of the family. Amara was a real Rossi and he could tell. A sudden qualm hit him—what if his father was right, what if he wasn't a real Romano? He shook the thought away, focused instead on Amara, saw her expression tauten. 'My grandfather brought me up. I lost my parents when I was four.' Her voice was even, didn't stumble or pause or break and he instinctively knew she didn't want to discuss it further. 'Since then, it has been him and me. Until now. Now it turns out that I have two half-siblings. Twins.' Now her voice did stutter slightly and he moved closer to her in the hope she would take comfort from his presence. 'They are two years older than me and they had no idea about their real paternity until recently. But when they found out they contacted my grandfather and testing has proved conclusively that they are…definitely family.' Her voice held a bewilderment that was almost tangible and he got that. Tried to imagine how it must feel. At least he and his half-brothers grew up knowing of each other's existence. Their relationship had been warped from the start and they now had no contact but at least that was through his own choice. He stopped, took both of her hands in his.

'That is a massive amount to take on.'

'My grandfather sees it as a positive—he

feels we have a moral duty to welcome them to the family. Which I agree with,' she added hastily.

'But you aren't feeling as positive as he is?' he said, picking his words carefully, keeping her hands firmly clasped in his when he sensed her about to pull back. 'It's okay. It's completely understandable if you have some reservations. You must be feeling…displaced.'

Surprise sparked in her eyes. 'That is it exactly. I feel pushed aside, unnecessary, outnumbered.'

'And angry.'

'Yes. You do get it,' she said softly. 'I feel as though I should go out, do something to fight back. When there isn't even a fight. That's hardly welcoming. And of course my grandfather wants to welcome his grandchildren, his flesh and blood, into the family. It's not a duty to him, he is looking forward to it, and I should feel the same way, should be happy for him. Because this solves everything really.'

'How so?'

'They may already be married or in long-term relationships, hell for all I know they may already have children. Ready-made heirs for the Rossi estate. I should be pleased—it takes the pressure off me.' She sighed. 'That's not fair. My grandfather has never pressured me to marry or have children. Ever. But of course, he is worried about the future of the Rossi estate. But I have always been happy to avoid the issue, avoid the topic. All this time it must have been bothering him—of course it must. I just wanted to pretend it was all okay.'

'Maybe it was okay. Maybe it is okay. There is still plenty of time for you to find a relationship.'

'No.' Her voice was quiet but absolute. 'I don't want that, I don't want a relationship, or to get married. It wouldn't work and I can't fake it. I don't want love. I like being on my own.' Gio heard the sincerity in her voice, an echo of his own sentiments on love and autonomy, wondered why Amara was so adamant. 'That's why I should be happy with the idea of these new people. But I'm not, because I know what I may have to do.' Now her voice was weighted with sadness and without thinking he stepped closer, so they were oh, so close.

'What?' he asked.

'I haven't admitted it until now, until saying it all out loud. My grandfather will make my siblings heirs, will want them to be involved in the estate. Assuming Lorenzo or Daisy or both of them grow to love the estate, I'll have to step aside. For the sake of the estate, for the sake of its future. There are two of them. If they are married there would be four of them. The decisions would be theirs to make. The estate will become their children's future, their legacy. They won't need me.'

And she wouldn't need them, the inference clear. 'I cannot believe your grandfather would want you to step aside.' Not from everything she had said about their relationship. Plus, it would clearly break Amara's heart to relinquish her place in the Rossi dynasty, to step aside from an estate she clearly loved. Yet she would do it. And Gio wasn't sure that made sense, wondered if there was something deeper going on.

'Of course he won't and as long as he is alive and wants me to, I will stay. But…the future has changed now. And I need to accept that and try to embrace it. For my grandfather's sake, for the estate's sake. That is what is most important.'

There was no doubting her sincerity and his heart twisted as he heard her attempt at positivity, at acceptance. 'Don't jump the gun too quickly. Your half-siblings may not be how you picture them. They may not even want to be involved with the Rossi estate. They may not consider themselves to be Rossis.'

'I cannot believe or wish for something like that. If that was the case, I would encourage them to be true Rossis to love the land and their new heritage as I do. For my grandfather's sake.'

A sense of admiration touched him and without thinking he reached out, and gently cupped her face in his hands. 'I don't know you very well, Amara, but from what you have said I can see how much you love your grandfather and your heritage. I believe you will do what is right and I hope that there is a way that means you don't lose what you love.'

He looked down at her upturned face, struck once again by how beautiful she was, though he couldn't quite pinpoint what it was about her that called so emphatically to him. Made him want to drown in the green depths of her eyes. But he wanted more than that. He wanted to help, to make the sadness in her eyes go away, to find a solution. He wanted to kiss her, distract her in a way he knew would chase her troubles away. Albeit temporarily. And he was almost sure that was what she wanted. *Almost.* Or perhaps Amara felt exactly what he felt; an overmastering attraction that she didn't want to feel.

He inhaled the fresh crisp cold air, relieved that it cleared his brain at least a little, as she gently pulled away from his grasp.

'Thank you, Gio.'

'You're welcome,' he said and now he did know what to do. A better solution to a kiss. 'And now I think it is time for some distraction.' From the gravity of her situation and from the attraction that threatened to overcome common sense.

'Agreed. Any ideas?'

'I do have an idea. Let's make a snowman.' He shrugged. 'Or a snowwoman.' For a moment he thought she'd scoff at the idea and then her face broke into a smile. 'It will use up some of our energy and it may even be therapeutic.'

'I like it,' she said. 'Let's do it.' Warmth touched him as her luminous green eyes lit with a sparkle. She scanned the landscape and Gio watched her, absorbed by the glint of sunlight on the waves of her reddish gold hair visible under her dark green woolly hat, on the slant of her brow faintly creased in contemplation. 'How about we make him over there.' She pointed. 'And we can find things for his face and body in that wooded bit over there.'

'Sounds perfect. I will follow your instructions. In fact—' and now his smile deepened '—your wish is my command.' There was a silence and they both stilled, their gazes locked, and he could see his own desire mirrored on her face. 'You just have to tell me what you want me to do.'

Her green eyes held his and what he saw in them ratcheted his pulse rate and it seemed to him the simmering attraction should be melting the snow around his boots.

'I'm not sure that's such a good idea,' she said softly, and then blinked and shook her head. 'I mean… I mean… I'm not really a snowman-making expert. But I'll give it a try.' Looking away from him she started to walk towards a flat bit of snow.

Gio knew he should feel relief that she'd broken the spell, severed the shimmering spark of connection, but he didn't. 'Let's get started,' he said.

Twenty minutes later they studied the sum of their efforts.

Gio had rolled a massive snowball for the bulk of the body and Amara had assembled two smaller ones.

'Right,' she said. 'Let's get them on top of each other.'

They both lifted the medium-sized snowball up and placed it carefully on top of the larger one, and Gio caught his breath. She was so close now, looking at him over the top, her face flushed pink with exertion, her eyes alight—and now tension strummed anew, and all he wanted to do was lean over and kiss her. But instead, he focused on picking up the head and placing it on top and then she walked round so they were next to each other, side by side, and he could feel the tautness of her body next to his, knew she was reining herself in the same way he was bracing himself, in case they should so much as accidentally brush hands. She leaned down and picked up the pine cones they'd found. Handed one to him.

Ten minutes later they stepped back and surveyed the finished product. Amara gave a spontaneous peal of laughter. 'He looks quite…'

He tipped his head to one side and looked at the arrangement of stones, twigs and cones that they had used to make his face.

'Frustrated,' he said without thinking.

Amara moved closer to him to see the snowman from the same angle. 'Oh,' she said. 'You're right.'

Gio couldn't help it, he gave a sudden crack of laughter and then Amara joined in and somehow, without him even knowing it they had turned to face each other and as the laughter died down, they were close, so close, her face upturned to his and…

This time he couldn't help himself. Couldn't stop something that felt so right, so inevitable. Without thinking he leant down, meant to simply brush her lips with his, no more. But as their lips met, the gentle fleeting gesture he'd intended ignited the spark that had been simmering since they'd laid eyes on each other.

Now she stepped forward into his arms and he tasted the lingering vanilla tones. Her lips parted and he deepened the kiss, and sheer pleasure flooded his veins, sent him to dizzying heights of sheer exhilaration. The taste of her, the exquisite passion of her response, the feel of her arms looped round his neck, the press of her body against his all combined to create a heady glorious tornado of sensation.

One that was too short-lived, even though it took at least a minute to identify the noise that was trying to penetrate the sheer density of the bubble of need and desire. Eventually his brain told him that it was a phone, his phone, the ringtone identifying the caller.

Amara must have heard the insistence of the noise because at the same time as he oh, so reluctantly broke the kiss she too stepped back, and even then, they stood staring at each other, until finally he reached into his pocket, tried to even his ragged breath. 'I—I have to take this.'

She nodded and he could see shock in her eyes as he moved away, his legs leaden as he exhorted his brain into gear, sought to shut out the rippling after-effects of a kiss that had blown his mind.

But he had to focus; his grandparents would not be calling him without good reason. They had understood he needed time and it wasn't Aurelio or Ava's style to pressurise him now. They'd agreed a week.

One more deep breath and he answered, looked down at the screen and his brain kicked in, showed him they had video called. He turned to angle the screen away from the glint of the sun and now he focused, saw the expression on his grandparents' faces.

'What's wrong?' he asked.

'Gio?' He could hear anxiety in Ava's voice. 'I…'

'It's okay,' Gio said and now foreboding touched him. 'Take your time. Is there a problem?'

Ava took a deep breath. 'Yes. There is. There is something we didn't tell you Gio.' She took a deep breath. 'I have been diagnosed with Alzheimer's.' Gio's chest contracted, the thought of the future caught at his heart. 'It is early days but…that is why we are standing back from the company. We want to spend the next years together, travelling, making the most of our time.'

'We told the family about your grandmother's condition,' Aurelio said, and Gio could hear the anger in his grandfather's voice. 'Salvatore said he knew something was wrong, that now he understood what it was, that he is ready to take over the reins. When we questioned his plans, he at first refused to discuss them, said that was no longer our concern. I said until we actually stood back it was very much our concern. I am afraid things went downhill from there.' Aurelio's voice held both anger and sadness and it hurt Gio to also hear a soupçon of doubt. Never before had he heard doubt in his grandfather's voice. 'His plans will ruin the company. Worse, he has threatened legal action, will question our capacity if we don't comply with what he wants.'

Gio tried to think of something comforting to say, but he couldn't, because to him this sounded like a typical bully's tactics. And his father was a bully. But what was worst of all was that for the first time ever Aurelio Romano looked vulnerable. And Gio understood why. The one person who Aurelio loved more than his company was his wife. Ava Romano was her husband's world and Ava Romano was ill and their only son was taking advantage of that. Threatening their world.

There was no way Gio was letting that happen. He would not allow his grandmother's final years to be further blighted. By Salvatore.

Memories flooded his brain. The silky tones of his father's voice as he explained why actually it was allowable, permissible for Max and Antonio to punish their brother for perceived wrongdoings. 'This is their house, Giovanni. They are my real family and you are merely a mistake. Therefore, if they ask you not to touch their toys you shouldn't.' Gio had tried to explain that he hadn't, that in fact, they had offered to let him play with one and only afterwards had they told him he should have refused. Salvatore had shaken his head. 'It is simply a lesson you must learn, Giovanni.' And so whatever punishment it was had been meted out. Perhaps he was asked to sit at a separate table during dinner, facing the wall. Or his brothers had made him do pointless exercises, push-ups or running on the spot. Or worst of all when he was small, the simplest thing, force him to sleep without a night light. And all the while his father had looked on. Until one day, his grandfather had stepped in. Had made the bullying stop.

But now Salvatore would turn those silky explanations onto Aurelio and Ava. Gio could imagine it. Would use the Alzheimer's as justification and threat. To wrest control under the guise of being 'real family'. *'You have Alzheimer's, therefore if I ask you not to interfere you shouldn't. It is simply a lesson you must learn.'* Or accept the punishment, the scandal, the legal wrangling, to wrest control.

Once Aurelio had saved him from Salvatore, now Gio would return the favour. Because it was the right thing to do. Ava Romano had been sentenced to such a heart-wrenching future; his grandmother deserved to enjoy every minute left to her, deserved for it to be as stress-free as possible, deserved to be able to stand back and spend the next years with her husband knowing that their company was safe. But it was more than that—if Gio was honest with himself he would enjoy taking his father down, showing Salvatore that Gio was a real Romano, showing him that finally Aurelio and Ava had decided he was 'real family' after all.

Because however much he genuinely cared for his grandparents he'd never been that to them. Until now.

'It's okay,' he said. 'I've got this. I will sort this out.'

After he disconnected, he inhaled the crisp cold air and it was as if each breath crystalised the sharp, ice-cold edges of his determination.

He headed back to Amara, saw that she had moved away from the snowman towards the wooded area where they had found the decorations for their creation. She was stood by a tree, her gloriously red hair a stark contrast to the snow-laden branches and the wood of the tree trunks. As he approached, she turned, and he saw concern in her green eyes, along with a lingering knowledge, a memory of the kiss they had shared.

'Is everything okay?' she asked. She studied his expression. 'Now *you* look angry.'

'I am,' he admitted.

'Can I help? You helped me earlier. I'd like to return the favour.'

'Actually, you can help.' Gio wondered if he should think this through more, decided he shouldn't. 'You could marry me.'

# CHAPTER FOUR

AMARA STARED AT HIM, wondered if she'd heard right, knew she had and a shaft of hurt pierced her—was he mocking her offer of help? Was he in some way she didn't understand mocking the kiss they'd shared? A kiss that for her had been…sublime. She had never been kissed like that, equally she'd never kissed anyone like that. It had been as though her life depended on it, as though she and Gio were the only people in the universe. Every nanosecond had increased the scale of pleasure until she hadn't been able to think of anything except never wanting it to end. Had wanted to escalate and prolong every feeling. Surely that couldn't have been one-sided. But if he wasn't mocking her, what could he mean? Was he joking?

Then she studied his expression, saw the shadows in his eyes and the pallor of his face and the now-grim set to his lips. Realised he was deadly serious.

'I don't understand.'

He glanced around, but she had the feeling he wasn't seeing the snowman they had been laughing over just moments before.

'I need a wife,' he said. 'And I'd like you to consider my proposal.' He raised a hand. 'I haven't lost my marbles or the plot. I told you I came here to make a decision. That was part of it.' No doubt seeing she didn't look any the wiser, he gave a small rueful smile. 'Okay. My grandparents are Aurelio and Ava Romano and they own and run Romano Confectionery.'

'Oh.' Amara stared at him, cast her mind back to the articles she'd read about Gio Romano. Most of them had been about Gio's romantic exploits, alongside his relationship to Luna Rocco; she did have a vague memory of the connection, but she had had no idea that he was a direct descendant.

'For various personal and business reasons my grandparents need me to join the board of the company. However, the articles of Romano Confectionery cite that all family board members must be married.'

'But that's…' Amara tried to find a word for it and settled for, 'Gothic. And surely that can be questioned in a court of law? Or can't your grandparents change the articles?'

'Perhaps, but that would all take time and we don't have time.' There was sadness and determination in his voice. 'This is the quickest, least complicated way.'

Amara felt her jaw drop. 'It may be quick, but getting married is hardly uncomplicated. Plus…' She was really struggling with this. 'You can't get married just because some articles demand it.'

'I can if it gets me what I want.'

'But why is it so important?' Questions were churning around her brain. Why did his grandparents need him to join the board now? Where was his father in all this?

'Because I want my grandparents to be happy, to live out their final years in peace, knowing their company is safe.' His voice was even, but it held steel and a sadness that touched her. 'My grandmother isn't well, is getting frailer.' His voice caught and she saw the pain in his eyes. 'My grandfather…for him the most important thing in the world is his wife, even more than the company they both love. But neither of them wants to see their company go under, or be absorbed by a huge conglomerate. Romano Confectionery is incredibly important to them.'

'And that is what will happen if you don't join the board?'

'Yes.' He hesitated and now his face hardened, the lips that an hour ago had wreaked such magic, formed a thin line. 'I believe so. When my grandparents decided to stand back, they handed over some shares and some control to my father. It turns out that he has made decisions that they fundamentally disagree with, is determined to do things his way, regardless of their wishes.' Amara heard cold anger in each syllable. 'My grandparents want me to stop him. They will give me enough shares to enable me to outvote him, but to do that I need to be on the board. So yes, I can get married just because the board demands it. So back to where we started. Will you marry me?'

Amara stared at him, and now she did understand. If Lorenzo and Daisy tried to destroy the Rossi estate she would do anything to stop them. Including marriage. But the idea was impossible. And even if it wasn't…

'Why me?' She shook her head. 'You don't even know me.'

Now Gio smiled. 'I get it sounds a little off the wall,' he admitted. 'But I think we can maybe help each other out. This is a deal, an arrangement that can benefit us both.'

'I do not need or want to be paid to marry you.'

'Good. Because that is not what I mean. I am not offering you money or love.'

She shook her head. 'There is nothing you can offer me. I'm not interested in marriage.'

'Aren't you?' Gio leant forward slightly, his brown eyes intent. 'If it was a marriage without love, a partnership, wouldn't that be a good thing? You'd have support when your half-siblings come on board, and it would make your grandfather happy.'

His voice trailed off, presumably because he'd seen her reaction as her mind explored the idea. Hypothetically of course; not as a serious proposition. Because it wasn't off the wall—it was so far out there, aliens were probably listening in.

But the thought crept in that there was a certain symmetry to this. Gio was getting married because he cared about his grandparents and his family company. Why shouldn't Amara do the same thing? She pictured Vittorio Rossi's face, could see the width of his smile, his happiness that she was settling down, that she wouldn't be on her own after his death. The hope for the future it would give him. It would also give Vittorio someone else he could welcome to the family and if for any reason Lorenzo and Daisy didn't work out there would be backup.

Vittorio wouldn't need Lorenzo and Daisy so much and it would put less pressure on Amara to welcome them, bond with them. In a way she knew she couldn't do. The very idea weighted her stomach. She remembered having a family. Remembered running through the castle with Luca, playing a game of make-believe. Her father reading them a story, her mother brushing her hair. And two days later coming home from the hospital, to a castle empty and bereft of her twin, her parents, her grandmother. The only noise the echoes of her own memories, the patter of feet, the laughter, the games. Only her grandfather and Amara left.

Because that was what could happen. Life could implode in a flash. Fate could wreak tragedy. Amara wouldn't put herself in fate's path again. There was no point forming bonds, forging relationships, letting people in.

But despite herself, another scenario snuck in, herself showing these unknown siblings round the castle, getting to know them, laughter, banter, a shared bond. An image she pushed down and out. She would go through the motions; she would do what she had to do for Vittorio's sake.

But now she thought about doing it with someone by her side. With Gio by her side. A person *on* her side in the formation of the new Rossi family dynamic. It would give her a sense of security.

A warning bell clanged in her mind. What happened to the idea of it was best to be alone? But that was the beauty of this. Gio would be by her side as a business partner. He would be an ally rather than a romantic partner. She wouldn't have to worry about whether she was doing things right, wouldn't have to worry she was letting someone too close. She would make the rules. She wouldn't have to change or compromise her life. She could remain on the Rossi estate, Gio could live…wherever he lived. They could spend as much or as little time together as they wanted. She wouldn't have to worry about hurting him, analyse how she was feeling. Most importantly, this would be an alliance that would reassure her grandfather, make Vittorio feel he wasn't leaving her alone.

Surely this would have all the advantages of a relationship and none of the downsides? No real commitment, nothing confusing or complicated.

Whoa… This was Gio Romano. She shook her head. 'What about your lifestyle?' she asked. No way could she even consider this. She couldn't face being humiliated by infidelity even if there was no love involved. The question flashed through her mind—had her mother known of her father's infidelity? Had he been perennially unfaithful or had it been a one-off, one mistake? How could she not have known? Perhaps she had been like Amara, unable to sift through the nitty gritty, the unspoken nuances and rules of relationships.

For a moment he looked confused and then understanding dawned and a flash of anger sparked his brown eyes.

Her eyes narrowed. 'It's a fair point,' she said. 'Because if I married you, even if it's an arrangement your reputation is now my business. And whilst I accept I am basing this on a few celebrity gossip articles, those articles have you down as a playboy.'

Now the anger left his eyes and he nodded. 'You're right. I owe you an explanation.'

He thought and then, 'First I accept that I am seen with a lot of women. But they are mostly first and often also last dates.'

Amara thought about this and frowned. 'So you reject them after one date and move on to the next?'

'In actual fact, they tend to reject me, or I

suppose you could say it is usually a mutual decision to not take things further. Because I never promise anything that I can't fulfil. For me the point of the first date is honesty, to lay down parameters, set out intentions.' His voice was clear, guilt-free.

'And what are your intentions? Or lack of?'

'That depends,' he replied. 'I make it clear that I have no intention of long-term commitment or marriage. But that my short-term commitment would be genuine.' He shrugged. 'Some of my dates have been happy with that, others have been less happy. Which is fair enough. I understand that for a lot of people a first date should at least have the potential to lead to the long term one day. Or what's the point?'

'What is the point?' Amara asked, aware that she was genuinely interested in his philosophy, even if she didn't see how it squared with his idea of getting married to her. Or getting married to anyone.

Now he smiled, a smile so full of promise that she had to force herself not to react, as her toes curled. 'A good time for both people where no one gets hurt,' he said simply. 'Companionship, great sex, a bit of a laugh and when you part no hard feelings.'

'And then on to the next woman?'

'Not straightaway,' he said. 'In the past two years I have probably had relationships with three women. I just happen to have dated a lot more. Hence my reputation.'

'So you're saying on *every* first date you go on you tell your date that you are only up for the short term? If they are good with that you proceed. If not then you don't.'

'Yup. I think it is fair to make it plain I don't want long-term commitment.'

Amara stared at him. 'I hate to point this out but marriage is a long-term commitment.'

This pulled a smile from him. 'I get that. But the reason I am averse to long-term commitment or a long-term relationship is because I don't want love. I don't want to run my life around an emotion that isn't predictable. I don't want to be ruled by an emotion. Unfortunately, most people believe that love is a prerequisite for marriage. If I do meet any women who don't, they seem to want to marry me for my money. I got the idea that you aren't interested in love or money. If I'm wrong then I take back my proposal.'

'You're not wrong. I meant what I said earlier. Love is not something I want. I don't want any commitment at all. And I certainly wouldn't marry you for money.'

'Then consider this marriage. I have no problem giving up my lifestyle, my string of first dates. I am not a heartless two-timing Lothario leaving a string of broken hearts in my wake. I have no wish to hurt anyone, or make any promises I cannot fulfil. I will only promise you what I can fulfil. Not love. But I can offer fidelity. Friendship.' His eyes met hers full on. 'Amongst other things.'

A shiver ran over her skin as the atmosphere morphed into something else and she tried hard to focus on the reality of this conversation. Yet she could hear the husk in her voice as she asked, 'What other things?' She gulped. 'Just to reiterate I am not interested in how much wealth you have.'

Gio waved a hand. 'That's not what I am talking about,' he said, and his voice deepened, held a promise that caught her breath. 'An attraction we know is off the Richter scale. The one kiss we shared was utterly mind-blowing so I am pretty sure we are…compatible.'

He drew out the syllables in a long drawl and she could feel her skin heat up under the deep rumble of his voice.

'One kiss doesn't mean we are necessarily compatible,' she managed to say.

'We could try another,' he offered and God help her she nearly leapt forward into his arms. Forced herself to remain still.

'Not a good idea,' she said firmly. 'We can't let attraction affect our decision-making here.'

'But it is a factor,' he said. 'If we are serious about this then the chemistry between us is crucial.'

'Then the question is, are we serious about this?' she asked as the sheer surrealness hit her. Was she truly contemplating marrying a stranger? 'I mean surely you must know women better suited for this than me.'

Gio shook his head, and his face was deadly serious now. 'No,' he said simply. 'This sounds a little off base, but it almost feels like fate sent us here at the same time. Two people mulling over two different problems, with the same solution. Marriage helps both of us. Two people who have similar views on relationships, two people who don't want love. That feels like fate to me.'

Fate. The idea made her feel edgy. After all, it had been fate that decreed that she had been the sole survivor of the helicopter accident that killed the rest of her family. It had been fate that decreed a last-minute crisis at the vineyard meant Vittorio hadn't been aboard. Now fate had brought her to the Bavarian Alps. All because one night over thirty years ago her father had been unfaithful to her mother.

'A set of random circumstances that meant we both meet at this point.'

'Yes,' he said and the syllable seemed to thrill through her. 'So yes, I am serious.'

She looked at him. 'How serious? I mean is this marriage something you need for a limited amount of time? I won't lead my grandfather up the garden path, sell him a marriage story only for it to fizzle out, end in divorce once you have your place on the board.'

'As far as I am aware no board member has ever got divorced. I have no intention of testing the principle, won't give anyone any ammunition to get me removed. Plus, I wouldn't do that to you. I will keep my part of the bargain—our marriage arrangement will remain in place until we make a mutual decision to end it.' He took both her hands in his. 'So, Amara Rossi. Will you do me the honour of marrying me?'

There were so many questions buzzing in her head, but in the end, this was the fundamental question and a sudden exhilaration gripped her.

'Yes. I will,' she said. And as she said the words, she felt a sudden surge of optimism, a sense that perhaps this could work. Because she would be in control, they could live by actual rules, terms, a contract. Things she did understand. 'What happens next?'

'We go back to the hotel and work out a plan.'

# CHAPTER FIVE

GIO HEARD THE knock on the door of his hotel suite, strode across to open it and felt a mixture of relief, disbelief and a strange warmth as he pulled the door open and saw Amara.

'I wasn't sure you'd come,' he admitted. She'd gone back to her room to change out of her hiking clothes and they'd agreed to meet and plan over lunch. 'I thought you may have changed your mind.'

'Nope. I do keep wondering if I am caught up in a dream or that perhaps this is some sort of prank, but I'm here.' Exhilaration raced through him and he could see that she felt the same way. Her green eyes held an element of shock but no doubts. That in itself buzzed through him. The idea that this could work. For both of them.

'I'm glad.' He stepped back and she entered, looked round the suite and her mouth opened. 'Wow,' she said.

He glanced round and grinned. 'You like it?'

'What's not to like? I take it this is step one in our plan.'

'Yup. We need privacy to plan, but we also need to start to be noticed. So, I requested a romantic lunch for two and the staff have really delivered.'

'They really have,' Amara agreed. She took in the roaring fire in the fireplace, flower petals spread across the table, the champagne in the wine cooler, the beautifully laid table and the elegantly presented food.

'I promised you fondue, so fondue you shall have.' They both surveyed the large pot of molten bubbling cheese. Flanked by plates with cubes of different bread, ready to be picked up with the gleaming silver fondue forks and dunked straight in. 'There's rye bread, pretzel bread, sour dough and good old-fashioned crusty white. I asked.' Because he knew she'd be interested.

'I'm betting the pretzel is amazing with the extra saltiness and the rye bread will give a real contrast.' She looked round. 'They've really thought about it. There are vegetable crudités which add the healthy touch and pickled vegetables, as well. I'm guessing the tartness of the pickle will give a bite against the creaminess of the cheese.' She gave a sudden laugh. 'Sorry. I have no idea why I am discussing food when we are here to discuss getting married.'

'Maybe because it seems a little surreal?' he suggested. 'And at least the food is real.'

'And will make a very memorable meal.' She pulled out her phone. 'If this is the start of our relationship, I think we should take some pictures for social media.'

'Bright and beautiful,' he said.

'What do you mean?'

'I mean you got it straight away.' She'd taken one look at the setting and figured out what he'd done and she was running with it.

'I guess I am a natural at faking it,' she said.

'I'll bear that in mind,' he said.

She closed her eyes and he grinned as her cheeks tinged pink. 'I didn't mean it like that…'

'You sure?' he asked.

Amara narrowed her eyes. 'This is *not* a conversation we should be having,' she said. 'We're here to plan what happens next.' She took a deep breath. 'Though…to be clear that doesn't include sleeping together. We need to make sure this is a good idea for other reasons than attraction. Sleeping together would complicate things and they are already complicated enough.'

'Agreed.' He met her gaze, wanted to reassure Amara that he got it. 'There's no rush. I don't want you to feel any pressure about that side of things.' There was also the sneaking suspicion that the attraction would be too all-consuming, too overwhelming and right now he needed to be focused on the big picture. On pulling off this marriage. He was pretty sure that his father wasn't going to go down without a fight and he needed to make sure he didn't win. 'We need to focus on getting this right and I know it's early days.'

'Exactly. It is early days. But we need to move fast, because you need to be appointed to the board as quickly as possible.' She paused. 'That means a quick marriage, which doesn't give us time to be absolutely sure this is a good idea. We both need to be able to change our minds, or change the terms and I think that will be more difficult if we are sleeping together.'

'Agreed.'

'Good. Now I'll take some photos then let's eat. I'm ravenous and this looks incredible.' Once she'd finished taking pictures of the table she glanced at him. 'I guess we'd better take a picture of us together. Our first selfie...'

He nodded. 'Hang on. I'll open the champagne.'

A few minutes later they were holding crystal glasses full of the pale sparkling wine. Amara held it up to the light that flooded in from the floor-to-ceiling window, and then took a tiny sip, before nodding in appreciation. 'Lovely. I wasn't sure about champagne and fondue but this will go really well. It's got a crisp floral tone that should complement the food beautifully.' Seeing that he was watching her, she bit her lip. 'Sorry. I think it's either a bad habit or a nervous habit.'

'Don't apologise. I really don't mind.' Truth be told he already liked it, the small frown of concentration that creased her forehead, the way she crinkled her nose slightly as she tasted the wine. The thought that went into her verdict.

She gave a small smile, but he was pretty sure she thought he was just being polite. 'Let's get the photo.' She edged towards him and stopped. 'Actually, I feel a little silly. I mean it's a bit awkward. Are we supposed to look all lovey-dovey? That's not really my style, plus this is meant to be the start of our relationship, so perhaps we need to look more…dazed? I really have no idea how to do this.'

He put his glass down on the table and gestured to the window. 'Let's stand there so we've got all the snow and scenery behind us and then I guess we try to look relaxed and happy.'

One photograph later they looked at the result and Amara grimaced. 'We look like we're desperately trying *not* to touch each other or get too close.'

'That's because we are desperately trying not to touch each other.' By so much as a brush of the hands. 'And that's not going to work. We have to look as though we are comfortable together or none of our social media pictures will work. Or any subsequent publicity.' Gio wasn't a huge celebrity, but as Luna Rocco's son and as someone who had dated his fair share of celebrities, he was still worthy of some coverage. 'My idea is that anyone checking our social media will be sure to see a real credible timeline of our romance. And if we can get pictured tonight at some celebrity hangout then all the better. The more publicity we garner, the more open we are, the more authentic it will look.'

'So we need this photo to work,' Amara said.

'I've got an idea.' Gio wasn't sure if it was a good idea or not but what the hell. 'Whilst we're taking the photo think about the kiss we shared. Remember how it felt and maybe that will help.'

Doubt floated across her eyes and then she

gave a small shrug. 'Okay. Right, here goes.' She held her phone up and Gio thought back to earlier, remembered the feel of Amara in his arms, the taste of her lips, his hands pulling her closer, the press of her body against his.

'Done,' she said and her voice sounded as breathless as he felt.

They surveyed the photo. 'I guess that did it,' she said. 'We look…'

'Dazed,' he completed. 'And happy.' And he couldn't help thinking how happy they would actually both be if they repeated the kiss in reality. Bad idea. Because that would distract them from what they were supposed to be doing. 'Now that's done we'd better start figuring out exactly how this is all going to work.'

They sat down and picked up their fondue forks. He couldn't help smiling as he saw how carefully she chose which bread to sample first, the way she made sure the cube was perfectly coated in the fondue before tasting it. 'Good?' he asked.

'Incredible. Creamy with a kick of something. I reckon it may be mustard.' She chose the next cube and said, 'Right. Okay. After eating all of this, what happens next?'

He took a moment to appreciate the food himself before answering. 'After our social media blitz to set the scene for a whirlwind romance, we'll announce the engagement as quickly as possible. Followed by a marriage as fast as possible.' He was damned sure his father would keep him off the board until the marriage was watertight and would be plotting in the background. Assuming his father even considered the idea that Aurelio and Ava would bring Gio on board. There was a good chance he wouldn't even contemplate so fantastical a notion. Gio was finding it hard to get his head round the idea himself. Knew the only reason was the fact Aurelio Romano couldn't think of another play, had decided this was the only move that would save his wife and their company. Whatever the reason, it gave Gio a chance to repay the debt he owed his grandparents and show his father that he was a real Romano after all. And he had every intention of taking that chance. 'There will be nothing hole and corner about it. Love at first sight is the theme and it's a story we'll stick to. The whole thing should look like a fairy tale.' Because once his father did cotton on to events, he would look for any reason to challenge the marriage.

Amara thought for a while. 'The key is to make this believable so we need to show this is different from your usual relationships. But we need glamour too. I agree we need a bit of external publicity, not just generated by us.'

He sipped his champagne. 'I propose we head to Munich tonight, go to a celebrity-studded restaurant, get our photo taken, stay in a fancy hotel. Then we change it up. We'll go and spend a few days in a romantic chalet in the Alps. Maybe make it a bit of a road trip, stay in different places.'

'That makes sense. We could take it in turns to pick where we stay. If you book tonight's hotel I'll book tomorrow's chalet and so on.'

Gio nodded; he appreciated Amara's practical viewpoint and the fact she clearly saw this as an equal partnership.

She prodded a potato and carefully coated it in cheese. 'I will talk to my grandfather this afternoon.' There was a hint of worry in her voice. 'I think he will be happy and I hope he will believe the story. He and my grandmother had a whirlwind romance. He always describes it as a love tornado and they were happy for decades.'

He thought he saw wistfulness on her face and a qualm struck him. 'Are you sure about this? About marrying me. I know you said that you have no interest in relationships, but are you sure? Are you sure you don't want to hold out for love, a real happy ever after, something you can tell your grandfather is genuine?'

'I'm sure.'

'I need to know more than that. I need to understand so that I can be absolutely sure before we start the charade for real. I get you had a relationship that didn't work out, but that is hardly grounds for believing love isn't possible or that you don't want it.'

'It's more than that. I had two relationships that didn't work out. *You* don't want love because it's an emotion you can't control. I don't want it because I don't get it. And I can't. I can't see the point of it.'

'What happened with your exes?'

'I met Stefan at a wine-makers convention. We fell into conversation. It was the first time I'd gone without my grandfather and Stefan was very knowledgeable about wine and I suppose I was flattered when he asked me out. We started seeing each other. But it wasn't fun. It felt like hard work. I'd feel like I had to prepare all the time, plan, think about good topics of conversation, look right, say the right things.'

'But surely you could just be yourself?'

'That's exactly it. I couldn't. I couldn't work out how. Everything I said sounded silly. Stefan didn't like it if I overanalysed food or drink, he didn't like it if I spoke too much about wine. It felt as though he didn't like lots of things about me. But I'm not sure I was actually ever being me. The whole thing made me edgy, nervous. Stefan said I was too cold and he was right—I was. I couldn't relax.'

'Maybe Stefan wasn't right for you.' Gio couldn't help thinking the man sounded like a bit of a pretentious arse, but hey, what did he know. 'People shouldn't try to change other people in a negative way.'

'That's what I thought. Especially when he left me for someone else. But two years after, I met Silvio. He was really different from Stefan, nicer, kinder, but the same problems were there. I couldn't relax, I couldn't figure out how to behave. And he ended up frustrated because he really was a nice guy, but I couldn't seem to let him in. I was still always on edge. I never felt at ease. The whole thing made me… Anxious. And the harder I tried the worse it became. In the end I ended it because he deserved someone who could actually appreciate him. The whole thing made me realise that I'm not cut out for a relationship.'

'But however nice Silvio was he still may not have been right for you.'

'I don't want to meet someone who is right for me. That would make it even worse, even more scary. Make me even more worried if I'm doing the right thing. If I really cared about them, if I loved them, I'd be a wreck. I am way happier on my own, in my own space and solitude. I'm not interested in investing my emotions, my time, in all the anxiety love seems to require. So this arrangement works for me.' She tipped her head to one side. 'Come to that, how do *you* know you don't want love? And are you sure this works for you?'

They were fair questions and he took some time to marshal his thoughts, didn't want to give Amara a flip or glib answer. But he was sure. He'd spent his whole childhood reliant on other people's whims. People who didn't want him or love him. After his grandfather discovered the bullying, Gio spent one weekend a month with his grandparents and those had been his most treasured times, shared with people who chose his company. And during those visits, over the years they had forged a bond, had built a relationship, a mutual respect and a liking for each other's company. But Aurelio and Ava had never wavered in their belief that he shouldn't be treated as a true family member, shouldn't be allowed into the echelons of the company. Fundamentally, even his grandparents didn't truly want him, or accept him. But they at least made the best of him, the Romano they too saw as a 'mistake', a blip in the respectable traditions of the family, the child who should never have been born, from a marriage that should never have been made. A Vegas joke.

But now he would be having the last laugh. He was the one his grandparents had turned to, to take down the 'real' Romano, the pillar of respectability. And he would do it because he cared about them, because it was right, but there was no point denying that a part of him felt vindicated. Vindicated but still not loved. The knowledge sent a swirl of emotion through him, a sense of anger, but most of all a sadness.

*Enough.* He'd long ago accepted love wasn't coming his way, had spent his childhood wishing that someone wanted him, cared about him. He wasn't opening himself up to that again. And he wasn't allowing anyone else to control his life either, wouldn't act on someone else's whims.

So now he met Amara's gaze full on. 'I am sure this works for me and I am sure I don't want love. I like to live my life the way I want to live it. I don't want to answer to anyone else.'

'Is that how you see love, as answering to someone else?'

'Yes,' he said. 'Or at least it should be. It's a responsibility.' He'd never understood why his mother didn't feel responsible for him, didn't feel any maternal obligation to be there for him. 'If you love someone you should think about them, take their desires into consideration. I don't want to do that. I want to make my own choices.'

'That works for me. I don't want you to feel responsible for me and I am quite happy for you to make your own choices. Plus, if this does go all wrong neither of us can get hurt—that's the beauty of it.'

She raised her glass, and Gio followed suit, but as he did so, a sudden, small doubt that he couldn't pinpoint pinged at the back of his brain. A doubt he squashed. Amara was right—this was foolproof. They were both on the same page about love. This would work.

'To us,' he said.

'To us,' she echoed.

Amara pushed her hotel room door open and put her purchases on the bed. Thank goodness the hotel had a boutique. She glanced at her watch; she didn't have much time to get ready before they left for Munich. They'd decided to head straight to the restaurant for dinner and check into the hotel in Munich after their meal. Which had at least given her some time; time to get into character, time to do some shopping before they announced their relationship. Started the social media campaign.

She surveyed the clothes and hoped she'd made the right choices. She hadn't packed in the expectation of wining and dining with Gio Romano as his soon to be fiancée. The whole idea was still hard to wrap her head around, especially when she contemplated the glare of publicity she was about to step into.

Yet, truth be told, that hadn't been at the forefront of her mind when she'd been stood in front of the clothing racks. She'd been thinking about Gio, about the reaction she wanted to evoke; had pictured his brown eyes darkening with desire, gleaming with appreciation when he saw her.

And that was all wrong. It was the camera she was playing to, not Gio. This was a contract marriage and for all she knew it wouldn't actually work out. She liked the synergy, the idea that she was helping not just her own grandfather but also Gio's. But she still didn't fully understand the Romano family dynamics.

There were still so many questions, so much they didn't know about each other, and Amara knew she had to tread carefully, had to make sure the attraction didn't affect her ability to assess the situation. She, *they*, both needed clear heads. And she needed to remember that if the Romano dynamic changed Gio might change his mind. Come to that, he might change his mind full stop. He might spend a few days with her and decide it couldn't work. Stefan and Silvio had found her lacking. There was every chance Gio would too. Equally Gio might not be the man *she* believed him to be. After all, she barely knew him. It could be that the attraction was colouring her vision of the man; her hormones could be jamming her brain signals. That was why they had both agreed not to act on the attraction.

So maybe the dress she'd chosen for tonight wasn't a good idea.

Her phone rang just as she was contemplating a mad dash back to the shop.

Her grandfather.

Swiftly she picked up.

'Amara! I am returning your call. How are you? How is Bavaria?'

'It's all good, Nonno. Really good. Something…unexpected has happened.'

'Are you okay?' She could almost see him frowning. 'You sound different.'

'I'm going out for dinner with someone,' Amara said.

'You didn't need to call to tell me that.'

'I do. Because the man I am having dinner with is Gio Romano. He's not a celebrity or anything, but he is in the public eye a bit so there may be some publicity.' She knew her grandfather would go away and do some research, so she continued. 'I promise you, Nonno, he is not like the papers say, he is…' She paused, wanted to lie as little as possible. 'He is a good man, I know it. I…feel something I have never felt before. And he does too.' Neither of them had ever contemplated marriage before, that was for sure.

'I trust your instincts, Amara. I always have. But be careful.'

'I will, I promise. It's only dinner—it may lead to more or it may not. I just didn't want you to be surprised by the publicity.' Amara decided she had done enough for now. Sown the seeds for a potential engagement announcement as best she could. 'How is everything at home?'

They discussed work and then Amara asked

the question she'd been dreading, hoped that her voice was civil, interested, positive.

'Is there any news on Lorenzo and Daisy?'

'Yes. I am hoping to set up a meeting with Lorenzo for when you are back. I assume you will wish to be here.'

'Of course. I am planning on flying back in five days. Is…is he coming to Tuscany?'

'Yes. He will be on his own. We decided that was best. I believe he is quite protective of his sister.'

Amara realised her hand had clenched into a fist. Would Luca have been protective of her? What would life have been like if fate hadn't stepped in and doled out tragedy?

'That's wonderful,' she heard herself gush. 'Let me know the final arrangements. I'll be there.' Even if the very thought weighted her with dread.

Putting her phone down she turned back to the clothes laid out on the bed and suddenly all her earlier qualms seemed irrelevant. It was a dress. In the scheme of things it didn't matter if she wore it. After all, life could change within moments in ways it was impossible to fathom. In a few days' time she was going to meet a half-brother she could never have imagined existed. Just as Lorenzo Cavendish could never have imagined that he had a different father than he'd believed all his life. Then a little later she was planning to marry a man she barely knew. As part of a contract that would benefit them both.

So, she needed to play her part. Honour the deal she'd made. And the dress she had chosen would do exactly that. As for the reaction she hoped to provoke—well why not? As she got ready, wriggled into the dress, brushed her hair, swiped on what she hoped was the right amount of make-up, Amara had a sudden urge to seize the moment, to let Gio distract her from thoughts of Lorenzo and the forthcoming meeting. Why not play the part to the hilt? Make sure this whole fake relationship looked real.

Only it wasn't a fake relationship.

She was really going to marry him.

The thought sent a swirl of panic-laced anticipation through her as she heard the knock on the door. Knew it was Gio.

# CHAPTER SIX

GIO OPENED HIS mouth to say hello and realised no sound was coming out.

Amara looked… Utterly sensational. The dress was a gorgeous concoction of cascading sequins, that shimmered with the reddish-gold hues of a sunset, and fell in a glittering swirl to her calves. The tank-styled neckline showed the column of her throat encircled by a topaz necklace and her hair fell in silken waves past her shoulders, crying out to be touched. Hell, all he wanted to do was touch. To pull her into his arms and kiss the glossy lips, to inhale her scent.

Somehow, he managed to get his brain and vocal chords to connect. 'You look…breathtaking,' he settled for, and somehow, he knew he would never forget this vision of her.

'You look pretty good yourself,' she said, her voice low and shy and her eyes bright with desire.

'Thank you.' Dammit, desire was literally rendering him tongue-tied. 'The car's waiting downstairs.'

By common consent they walked down the stairs to the lobby; the idea of being confined in a lift simply too risky at this point. Gio wondered if there were sparks flying around them visible for all to see, and noticed they garnered a few looks as they walked across the marble floor.

Telling himself he was using the moment, he took her hand in his, felt a shock wave course through his body, saw her step falter slightly. Turning, she looked up at him, her eyes flecked with desire, her lips slightly parted.

Once outside they both inhaled sharply as if in hope the cold night air could shock them. Then he opened the door to the chauffeured car he'd organised to take them to Munich.

'You're definitely making a statement,' she said, as they waited for their luggage to be collected and put in the boot.

'I'm aiming to get us noticed. The restaurant should get us some publicity, as well. There are usually photographers lurking to get some celebrity pictures. Will that be okay?'

She thought for a while as the car started its journey. 'I think I'll be fine. Over the years I have been the face of Rossi wines. I manage our PR and I've done some talks. It's terrifying, but I'm good at pretending. I imagine a wall between me and other people. It's a wall that protects me—it keeps me safe. It's like a knowledge that no matter what happens it's not a worst-case scenario.' She frowned. 'I'm not explaining myself very well. I always think what is the worst thing that can happen? I can make a mistake. People could laugh at me. I could drop a bottle of a wine. I could taste a Bordeaux and say it's a merlot.' She gave a quick smile. 'But I can come back from all those things. What's the worst that can happen tonight? They get an unflattering picture of me? That wouldn't end the world. The worst I can lose is a bit of pride or dignity.' She smiled at him and he saw a wealth of sadness in her green eyes and his chest twisted. He guessed nothing could be worse than losing your family in one fell swoop. If you'd lived the worst-case scenario you would be able to not get too involved in the angst of social situations.

He shifted slightly closer, hoped he was conveying some comfort or reassurance and they completed the journey in a silence that felt comfortable, both of them lost in thought until the car glided to a halt.

'We're up,' he said. 'You ready?'

'I'm ready. The wall is up.'

A wall that held the world at bay and kept her safe. Safe from caring about the things so many people cared about. He got that. And that created a sense of connection along with a reassurance that this marriage idea really could work. Because Amara was safe behind her wall and he was equally safe behind his.

As they emerged from the car, he took her hand in his, again felt that zing and jolt of sheer electricity, enough to light the way towards the renowned restaurant, the haunt of the rich and famous.

He saw the flash of cameras, sensed the buzz, felt her slow down ever so slightly, not enough to call it an invite for attention but enough to allow them to be seen. Then she turned and looked up at him with a smile that lit her face and he leant down and brushed her lips with his, a clear signal to the onlookers that they were a bona fide couple.

He felt the shiver run through her and it was only the knowledge that they were in public that stopped him from deepening the kiss, and as they walked in it was increasingly hard to focus on saying the right thing to the staff who met them, to keep a smile on his face, to try and look suave and charming when all he wanted to do was tug her hand and race out of the restaurant and on to the hotel. Where they were sharing a two-bedroom suite he reminded himself.

As they sat down opposite each other she smiled at him, reached over and covered his hand. ‘So far so good,’ she said softly and turned her attention to the menu.

She was still looking when the waiter returned. ‘I’ve brought some complimentary hors d’oeuvres and a glass of champagne.’

‘Thank you. Could I have a little more time to look at the menu?’

‘Of course.’

‘Hmmm…’ He heard the small sigh she gave as she looked back down, the crease of concentration on her forehead. ‘How on earth can I choose?’ she said. ‘This is all…amazing.’

‘There’s no rush,’ he said. ‘I’m quite happy sitting here watching you choose.’

She shook her head. ‘No way. You can’t order whatever I do again.’

‘Why not?’

‘Because we have to choose different things. That way I get to taste more things. But no way am I doing that cringy couple thing where you feed each other bits of food.’

'Cringy?' He raised an eyebrow.

'There is nothing good about two people feeding each other in a cutesy way.'

'It's supposed to be quite enjoyable,' he said.

'Are you speaking from experience?'

'No. I have never fed anyone anything. But… we've got the perfect food to give it a try.' He gestured to the beautifully presented plate of appetisers.

She glanced at the selection. 'It almost seems a shame to eat them,' she said. 'They look incredible, I mean they are even colour-coordinated. Each one is a work of art.'

'All the more reason to use them for the camera. It's what couples do.'

She looked at him suspiciously and he grinned, won an answering smile. 'Go on. I reckon it may be… Interesting. Close your eyes.'

'I'm not sure. I don't really like surprises. I like my food in a certain order. Plus, not knowing what I'm about to eat is a bit unnerving.'

'Trust me.' There was a pause and he realised in some ways the words had a deeper meaning. Because all this was about trust. They were trusting each other. He was trusting her not to go to the press with the whole fake marriage idea; she was trusting him to sustain an illusion of love for the sake of her grandfather. 'I'll make good choices. And if I don't, you can tell me.' Honesty was the basis of their deal, after all, and without love, without that constant worry of losing it that would be easy.

Her gaze met his, then she gave a small nod and closed her eyes. He looked down at the food, picked a caviar-topped blini.

'So first up I am going to choose something light and delicate. A creamy, slightly briny flavour that brushes over you gently, and leaves you wanting more.'

He saw her gulp slightly, saw the rise and fall of her chest, wondered how wise this was. But he couldn't help himself. Carefully he put it into her mouth, just let the tip of his finger brush against her lip and desire twisted his gut as he saw the shiver run over her skin.

'It's lovely, the topping is slightly nutty as well, the whole thing is nuanced. It feels like I'm floating.'

'Now try this.'

This time when he put the morsel of smoked salmon canapé in her mouth, he'd swear she oh, so lightly nipped his finger, leaned towards him slightly. And his breath hitched, caught in his chest.

'This one has a smokiness and a tang of spiciness. A jolt to the senses.'

'Like this?' he asked.

And now he ran a finger over the palm of her hand, his thumb making small circles as she caught her breath.

Her eyes flew open, dark and dreamy with desire. 'My turn. Close your eyes.' Her voice was low and slow; it seemed to slide over his skin heating it up.

He closed his eyes and he felt her gently rub his lips, tasted the fizz and bubble of champagne.

'Taste the bubbles, how they fizz over you with a vanilla overtone and let the taste linger. Savour the unique blend that makes it explode in your mouth.'

Now he opened his eyes and their gazes locked and it truly felt like there was no one in the room except them, the hustle and bustle seemed to have faded to mere background noise and all he could see was Amara.

Until awareness trickled in and he realised the waiter was now stood by the table. He blinked, knew he had to get things back in focus, saw Amara visibly pull herself together as she picked up the menu, smiled up at the waiter and made a choice. Gio followed suit, made a random choice, his interest in food minimal, his whole being still swirling with desire.

Once the waiter had gone they simply stared at each other.

'Um… I'm not really sure what to talk about,' she said.

'That's because it's quite hard to actually string a sentence together.' He ran a hand through his hair and tried to think. 'Tell me about wine,' he said. 'Maybe it will refocus us on conversation.'

'It's worth a try,' she said. 'Unless I bore you to death.'

'You won't do that.'

Though he did expect her to launch forth into a blitz of technical information or how grapes ferment, but instead she said, 'I think what I love best about wine is its history, how people were drinking wine millennia ago, not centuries but millennia.'

Her voice held awe. 'And I suppose I love that I am a cog in the whole history of wine. Did you know that it is probable that wine was first made in China in 7000 B.C.? I mean, that is mind-blowing. I am not sure how it was done, but I think honey and fruit were fermented to make alcohol. The idea spread to Georgia and then Persia, over the next two thousand years. And it was then that grapes were first used.'

'That is pretty amazing.' Gio thought for a minute. 'I mean, I can't even picture what people looked like back then, what they were wearing, but they were drinking wine.'

'All over the world. The ancient Egyptians even "bottled" theirs in jugs by labelling them with the year the wine was made and who made it.'

'And when did wine come to Italy?'

'In about 4000 B.C., most likely to Sicily. But it was all a bit haphazard until around 800 B.C. when the Greeks arrived. They brought vines with them and more importantly, they had a system—they organised things and brought their techniques and equipment and that's when it all really started.'

She broke off as the food arrived, waited for the dishes to be carefully placed and the wine poured and then glanced at him. 'Sorry I *have* been wittering on. You should have stopped me.'

'I didn't want to.' He knew the words to be utterly true. His interest in the topic was genuine, but he'd also been absorbed by her sheer seriousness, her passion for what she was talking about. The way her hands moved, her eyes sparkled, the way she leant forward to emphasise her point, the sound of her voice.

'And the Rossis have made wine for hundreds of years,' he recalled.

Amara nodded, a fleeting look of something he thought may be surprise on her face. As though she was surprised he remembered. Then she smiled, a smile that lit her face. 'I guess that's why I feel so involved. We are part of the Italian wine heritage and history. I've been part of it since I took my first breath. I was even born on the estate. It's in my blood and I love it. When you see it, I think you'll know what I mean.'

'Tell me about it.'

And as they ate, she did and he could almost see the rolling landscape, meadows scattered with wildflowers, a rugged, turreted stone castle with an ancient steepled chapel in the background. Cypress trees, olive groves and of course the stretch of vineyards, the vines going through the seasons from the unfurling buds of spring, the growth and ripening of summer and then autumnal harvesting when the vines change colour and the grapes were picked and then the winter where the vines regrouped and rested. And as Amara spoke, he could see that she was at one with the estate she'd grown up on, would cultivate and nurture each vine as though it had a personality, an individuality.

'But enough of me,' she said, breaking off with a self-conscious smile. 'What about you. Where do you live?'

'I move around a lot for business but I'm based in Milan. I've got an apartment there and I've also got a place in LA where quite a lot of my business is.'

'Tell me about your company. I know you are phenomenally successful and I know you are a med-tech entrepreneur, but I don't really know the details.'

'I designed an app that allows home health monitoring, so it can help patients with existing issues keep an eye on their health and allows everyday people to monitor various things. So people who are worried because they know they are at high risk of say heart disease, can monitor some of their risk factors.'

Amara tipped her head to one side. 'What inspired you to do that?' she asked.

He shrugged. 'I always had a bent for technology and engineering and I was interested in health. My grandfather had a heart attack when I was in my teens.' Gio could remember the shock he'd felt. To him, his grandfather had been invincible. And underlying the shock and the worry had been a craven fear that without the protection of his grandfather, his brothers, his father, would once again have power over him. Along with a sense of exclusion—he'd only found out about the heart attack weeks after the event. Hadn't been involved, was on the fringe of events.

He'd suppressed the thoughts, hated himself for his own cowardice and selfishness and perhaps from that had come the seed of an idea.

'I think that spurred me on and I came up with the concept and then I managed to get proper backing and it took off.'

'You make it sound easy.'

'It wasn't easy, but…' He hesitated. 'But I was so driven that somehow even when I got knockbacks, even when things went wrong, it never occurred to me that I wouldn't succeed.' Failure hadn't been a possibility. Because he'd had too much to prove. To himself and every single Romano, whether he loved or loathed them. That he could make it on his own, forge his own success.

He realised that he'd put way too much emotion into his voice, saw her green eyes looking at him with scrutiny and an understanding that made him edgy because he sensed a connection he wasn't sure he wanted.

'You definitely succeeded and I am guessing that you love your company, just as your grandparents love theirs.'

'Yes, I do. And I'm proud of the product we supply. I've got plans to branch out into other med-tech areas. There is so much out there now, so many things worth investing in, putting money into that can truly make a massive difference to people's lives. AI tech, robotics. Our R&D department is huge, and I also try to help out as many startups as I can. I also want to help places and communities that don't usually benefit from this type of technology, make it more accessible and affordable.' He broke off. 'Now I *really* am wittering on.'

'You really aren't. I can hear how much this means to you and how important it is. It sounds incredible and a pretty full-on job. It's also a very different industry to chocolate. Also…' She hesitated and he gestured with his hand.

'It's okay. You can say what you think.'

'I was curious. What made you set up your own company? And why an industry so different from chocolate? I mean you must have always known you'd end up at Romano Confectionery?'

Gio shook his head, knew that it was another fair question and that Amara deserved a fair answer.

'My parents' marriage was incredibly brief. It wasn't even real apart from in a legal sense. They got married in Vegas on some sort of drunken dare. Their whole relationship only lasted a matter of weeks, a brief aberration in both their lives. They annulled the marriage a few days after the Vegas ceremony. My father quickly remarried and my stepmother, Bianca, was already pregnant when my mother announced her own pregnancy. To my grandparents, I was the equivalent of illegitimate and they are old-fashioned enough for that to count. Respectability is important to them. They were moral enough to believe my father must acknowledge me and spend time with me. My mother insisted I took the Romano name.' Gio suspected she had done that quite simply to annoy the strait-laced disapproving Romano clan, had done it to emphasize her insistence on joint custody. Financial support hadn't been a consideration for either party, his mother was a multimillionaire in her own right and the Romano wealth was immense. But his mother had not wanted to be lumbered with a child full-time and his father hadn't wanted to be lumbered with a child at all. So, the fight had been over who could care for him the least. 'But although I would bear the Romano name, spend time with my father, I wouldn't be part of the Romano business. That would go to my father and then my half-brothers.'

'They excluded you? From the company that means so much to them?' Gio heard the shock, the outrage in her voice. 'So, you had to grow up watching your brothers being welcomed into the family business that you were barred from.'

'Yes. But…'

Amara shook her head. 'I know it is none of my business and I'm sorry if I'm overstepping, but what they did wasn't fair. And it isn't fair now for them to ask you to put aside your own business, your own global success to… To bail them out. Maybe you should think twice before joining the Romano board. Before getting married. I am doing this because the Rossi estate, my grandfather—they have been there for me all my life. I do owe my grandfather something, a marriage, a comfort and reassurance that I won't be alone. But from what you've told me I am not sure why you owe your grandparents anything.' He could hear a suppressed anger in her voice. 'What they did wasn't fair.' Another breath. 'You don't have to do this.'

Surprise slammed into him as he realised that Amara was actually incensed on his behalf. The knowledge twisted something in his chest and sent a warmth over him—after all, for most of his life no one had taken up the cudgels on his behalf.

Except, he reminded himself, except for his grandparents. But he couldn't tell Amara about the bullying. There was nothing to be gained by explaining or reliving past humiliations. Admitting weakness and guilt. Because sometimes in the recesses of his soul Gio wondered if it was his fault. After all, Salvatore appeared to care about his wife and his other sons. Maybe it was all just him.

But he knew he owed his grandparents. Not only for ending the torment, but for continuing to see him, for making him feel wanted, however briefly. But also, because Gio was the catalyst that had brought out and exposed Salvatore's worse traits. And that must have hurt Aurelio and Ava, to believe ill of their only son, their pride and joy. Their heir. And somehow, Gio had felt it was all his fault and he'd never once told another soul about what had happened.

Yet, as he studied Amara's face, he was almost tempted to tell her. Almost. Abruptly he shook the feeling off.

'I want to do this, Amara. Even though I was excluded from it I do love Romano Confectionery and I do care for my grandparents. I want to help them. They did what they thought was right and they showed me affection. And now, when they are old and frail, I won't turn my back on them. I want to do this.' He hesitated, and then honesty compelled him. 'And I want to show them that I can do this, that I am a real Romano.' He regretted the words as soon as he said them; knew he'd given away too much. Gave a shrug that he hoped would lighten his tone, hurried on. 'I suppose I'd like to make a point. But any which way, I want to do this. I want to marry you.'

There was a short silence and then she smiled. 'Then let's keep this show on the road.' She hesitated. 'I told my grandfather earlier that you are a good person. And you are.' And with that she leaned across the table, and with the lightest of touches she brushed her lips across his. And he knew that it was an affirmation that they were going forward; it felt different to the kiss before. This was sweeter and lighter and there was a shimmering strange sense of connection.

It engendered a warmth that set a warning bell off in the back of his head. One he sensed that she could hear, or perhaps her own thoughts followed his. Her green eyes stared at him as she sat back and she lifted a hand to her lips. Then, as if she was allowing the clatter and clink and surrounding conversation in, she blinked and she smiled but it was a smile that still left her eyes holding a hint of confusion.

Reaching out he raised his glass. 'To us,' he said softly. 'Our joint venture may not be easy but we are going to succeed.'

'To us,' she echoed, and somehow as their glasses clinked, the ring of crystal hitting crystal seemed to reverberate through the air, and the words took on a significance that echoed around them.

They placed their glasses down almost in perfect synchronicity. Their gazes met and he wondered if it was possible to drown in the green depths of her eyes. Knew he had to break the spell before he lost perspective. 'Dessert?' he asked, aware his voice was almost a croak.

She shook her head and he saw her hand clench round the edge of the table. 'I'm not hungry.' She took a deep breath. 'But maybe we should have something. Stay a bit longer.

We mustn't forget we're being watched, putting on a show.'

The reminder exactly what he needed; right now, the most important thing was pulling this off.

Making it look real. Not making it actually real.

# CHAPTER SEVEN

AMARA COULDN'T REALLY even remember what dessert they had eventually chosen; somehow the kiss, though it had been so brief, had evoked a slow burn of desire and now that the driver had dropped them off and they were stood in front of the hotel, she tried to clear her brain. Gio had clearly chosen the place for its opulence and she forced herself to focus on the building itself, the sprawling edifice in the centre of Munich a mixture of historic and modern architecture with its neoclassical exterior. As she stared at the arched windows, she hoped it would ground her, reduce her pulse rate, force her to remember that all of this was an act. Only it wasn't, was it? The attraction was definitely extremely real and it felt as if everything was moving at warp speed.

She'd given Gio a chance to opt out and maybe she'd really believed that he would take the option. Until now, there had been a bit of her sure that the momentum would stop, but now… Now she knew Gio was serious. The momentum was going to keep on keeping on.

Which made it even more important to at least slow something down; to ensure they didn't act on the attraction.

'Are you okay?' he asked.

'I'm good. Ready to check in and play my part.' That was the key. This was a part. There was no actual whirlwind romance, the dinner had been for the cameras. It was important to keep reality and fiction separate.

They entered the sweeping high-ceilinged marble lobby and approached the stretch of the sleek reception desk.

'Mr Romano, Ms Rossi. We have assigned you the deluxe suite on the top floor.' Amara smiled, still oh, so aware of Gio, aware too of the interested glances and she could only hope she was carrying this off. She felt Gio's hand encircle hers and a sudden reassurance touched her, one that lasted all the way up the elevator and as they entered the suite.

Once inside she took in the expanse of the room, the walls adorned with canvas pictures of Munich, the grained wooden floors dotted with bright rugs and colourful leather sofas. A sleek chrome desk ideal for business was placed under a large window and a state-of-the-art television covered another wall. The whole room exuded luxury. A sudden reminder of how much money Gio actually had.

But that wasn't what was making her feel awkward; the awkwardness came from the idea that the suite was made up of an opulent lounge and a no doubt equally opulent bedroom.

'Um…about sleeping arrangements,' she said.

'There are two bedrooms,' he said. 'There's an adjoining room through there.' He gestured towards a door.

Relief swathed her. A short-lived relief as it happened. Because…

'That's great and I really appreciate that. But…' Amara took a deep breath. 'I'm not sure separate bedrooms will work. Not because I don't want separate bedrooms,' she added hurriedly. 'But…'

For a second he looked puzzled and then the penny dropped. 'Of course. The hotel staff will clean the rooms and they'll realise we aren't sharing a room.' He thought for a moment. 'It's fine. I'll sleep on the sofa. I can take a pillow and duvet from the bedroom and that will be fine.'

Amara opened her mouth to agree and then

reluctantly shook her head. 'We could do that. But…it's still risky. Someone may knock on the door and we'd have to scramble to hide everything. Plus, the staff will notice the pillow and blanket have been used. I am pretty sure I've read about reporters paying hotel staff to check celebrities' rooms really carefully. I know that's probably unlikely but we have to make sure we look legit.'

'How?' he asked.

The million-dollar question. Gritting her teeth Amara said, 'We could share the bed. I'm betting it's king-size so there's plenty of space. That way if anyone knocks on the door or there is an emergency it will all look…authentic.'

'Are you sure it's a good idea?'

'No. In fact, I know it's a terrible idea. But if we're going to do this, we need to do it properly and let's face it, realistically there are going to be lots of occasions over the next weeks where we will be expected to share a bed.'

He nodded, though she could see the tension in his jaw. 'You're right. You go ahead then. I'll do some work and creep in later.'

Amara opened her eyes and stifled a gasp. Last night, sheer exhaustion had finally sent her to sleep before Gio had come in. She'd been tempted to pile cushions down the middle of the bed but had resisted the idea as unworthy. At best it was juvenile, at worst it would imply a lack of trust in Gio or worse a lack of trust in herself. She was an adult and quite capable of respecting Gio's space, as she trusted him to respect hers.

After all, she'd always believed that it was the person that mattered more than the attraction and yet with Gio the attraction threatened to overcome that belief. Overcome everything but the urgent need to give into the desire.

To lose control.

She did believe he was a good man, but she wasn't willing to do that. Instead, she dropped into slumber, clutching the edge of the bed to prevent herself from falling out.

But now…she held her breath as her brain took in what had happened. Somewhere in the night she'd stopped clutching the edge of the bed, burrowed across the king-size space she was supposed to be *respecting* and now she seemed to be clutching Gio. *Somehow*, she was right next to him, one arm slung over his chest, *oh God*, his *bare* chest. And now she was thinking in italics and praying he wouldn't wake up. But her treacherous mind was also wondering exactly what Gio was wearing. Her body was on high alert, was oh, so aware of the hard muscle under her arm, the rise and fall of his chest, all too aware of an urge to run her hand downwards, to explore, to shift even closer to him.

Instead, with excruciating care, she shifted infinitesimally away and instantly Gio's eyes opened, looked directly at her, though sleep still clouded the brown depths. Then he smiled, it was a sleepy smile that held sweetness and the remnants of dreams. Dreams that Amara suspected had run along the same lines as her own, dreams where touching was allowed, *welcomed.* Then his smile widened and in one automatic move he had somehow scooped her up so she was straddling him and she caught her breath as white-hot desire swooshed through her and then she saw sleep blink from his eyes and he swore.

Then 'I'm sorry. Hell, Amara, I didn't mean…'

Hurriedly she scrambled off him. 'It's okay. It's not your fault. It's not anyone's fault. I knew I should have used pillows!' Finding a pillow, she grabbed it and hugged it to her, surveyed Gio over the top and suddenly his face creased into a grin and without even thinking she chucked the pillow at him.

'It's not funny,' she said, even as a chuckle escaped her and then he caught the pillow and threw it straight back at her and they both began to laugh.

Eventually they subsided and Gio smiled and it took every single bit of willpower not to throw herself at him. And as their gazes met, she saw the warmth of his smile deepen into a heat, a desire and they were so very close and…from somewhere, she managed to move away.

'Right,' she said. 'We'd better get up.' And she hoped there wasn't even a hint of question in her voice, knew that now if he reached out and tumbled her over, she wouldn't even try to resist. But instead, she saw him tense.

'Sure.' He swung himself out of bed and Amara gulped, shoved her hand under her thighs in a reminder she couldn't, *mustn't* touch. He was wearing pyjama bottoms, but his chest was definitely a hundred percent bare and in full view. She watched as he reached down and tugged on a T-shirt, watched the stretch and movement and ripple of muscles and hoped, really hoped, she wasn't making little mewling noises.

'You can use the bathroom first,' he offered and she nodded, not trusting her voice. Not trusting herself. All she could hope was that a shower would bring her to her senses.

Half an hour later she emerged, feeling at least marginally more in control now that she was dressed in dark blue jeans and a dark terracotta knitted jumper.

Gio was sat at the table, his laptop open. 'We've made a good splash,' he said indicating the screen and she was relieved at his matter-of-fact tone, aware of a tacit consent to put the morning behind them. 'We're dotted over social media and there's plenty of curiosity as to your exact identity. Only a couple of particularly enterprising reporters seem to have worked it out for sure.' He rose. 'Have a read. I'll use the bathroom then I have a breakfast plan for our campaign trail.'

'Perfect.' As Gio headed to the bathroom her phone pinged and she saw it was a message from her grandfather. Sitting at the table, she looked to see what he had said, kept the screen open in front of her so she could see what Vittorio may have seen.

Dear Amara, I am glad you warned me about the incipient publicity—it was lovely to see you enjoying yourself and I hope good things come of this holiday. I look forward to seeing you in a few days. We will show Lorenzo the Rossi estate in all its winter glory. Nonno

Amara felt her tummy clench and instinctively she turned her screen off, sat for a few minutes staring sightlessly out of the window, oblivious to the hustle and bustle of the Munich street below.

'Amara?' She heard Gio's voice and blinked, pulled herself into reality, a reality that felt suddenly bleaker. 'You okay?'

'Sure. Ready to go.' She knew her voice sounded overbright and she looked away from him as they made their way to the door, then down into the lobby. On automatic, she managed to smile as they checked out, and then headed down to the car park to the car, climbed in and clicked her seat belt on.

Forced herself to focus on the job at hand; there was no point thinking about what was happening in four days' time when there was so much happening right now. But it was hard not to let the images seep into her brain and for a while she watched the blur of the snowy landscape, the splashes and colours of other vehicles, listened to the almost imperceptible hum of the car engine.

'Here we are.' Once they were stood in the

parking area, he looked around. 'This way,' and he gestured towards a horse and carriage stood a few yards away. 'Your carriage awaits,' he said. 'We're going to have breakfast at a castle,' he added as she climbed up into the open-air carriage and a gentle whirl of snowflakes flurried down from the sky in a magical cascade. Amara was content to remain silent as they clip-clopped along the road, surrounded by snow-laden trees and the sound of the horse's hooves, muffled by the blanket of snow, the jingle of the reins a musical accompaniment until twenty minutes later they arrived at their destination.

'You alight here and there is a viewing platform, then it's a ten-minute walk to the actual castle,' the driver told them.

They headed to the platform and Amara gasped. Multiple turrets and spire-topped towers soared to the sky, the whole building a romantic, magical, almost exaggerated fairy tale image, a mix of Gothic and Byzantine style that brought images of chivalry, dragons and sunsets to mind.

'It's like a fairy tale brought to life. Not that I believe in fairy tales,' she added quickly. The last thing she wanted was for Gio to think she had even a shred of romance in her.

He shrugged and the movement distracted her. Her eyes watched the lift of muscle; the breadth and strength and heat warmed her body. 'I don't believe in falling in love, but I do intend to live happily ever after.' His voice sounded deep and sincere and now he took her hand in his. 'That's the point of this marriage just as much as in a more conventional one. For us to live happily ever after.'

'But not together,' she said. 'Because we will both be individually happy, but our happiness won't depend on the other person. Our marriage is a…framework, an arrangement where we will spend some time together at the start, but as time goes on, we will naturally evolve to more separate lives.' Which was ideal for her, would allow her to retain her solitude, keep her safe from the anxieties and risks that came with a fairy tale happy ever after. You couldn't lose what you didn't have.

'Exactly.' His voice held satisfaction, one she shared wholeheartedly and yet as she looked back up at the castle Amara felt a strange sense of wistfulness, wondered what it would feel like to be the type of person who could actually feel love, the sort of person who could cope with that heady wave of emotion, could believe in fairy tales where the happy ever after was all about love and romance.

But that wasn't possible. She wasn't that person and she knew now she never could be. She'd tried—with both Stefan and Silvio, she'd tried. Hoped that somehow, she'd be able to do it, to experience closeness, love, a family. All the things she'd lost. But after the experience of those relationships, she knew it wasn't within her to get close to anyone or let anyone close to her. The wall was there, built of impregnable bricks of sorrow and knowledge and pain. She'd seen that happy ever afters could be crushed, wiped out, seen and experienced the sear of loss and grief. Could still remember her four-year-old self witnessing her grandfather's sorrow, a sorrow that she knew he still carried in him.

She turned to look at Gio, told herself that this arrangement was something she was capable of and dammit she would be happy. Without love. Behind her wall.

'Shall we walk up?' Gio suggested. 'I've booked a private tour and breakfast for us before the castle officially opens to tourists.'

Ten minutes later they arrived at the entrance, where a woman approached them, a smile on her face. 'Welcome,' she said. 'I'm Claudette. As we arranged, breakfast has been prepared for the two of you.' She smiled at Amara. 'We don't normally do this but Mr Romano was very persuasive. There are no working kitchens in the castle, but we have done our best. First, I'll show you some of the inside of the castle and then all we ask is that you finish in an hour so we can clear away and be ready for when the castle opens.'

'Of course.'

They followed Claudette and for the next half an hour Amara lost herself in the sheer magic of the castle's interior. Exquisitely detailed frescoes depicted ancient mythological tales, stained glass windows glinted and refracted shades of red and blue and delicately ornate chandeliers hung from numerous ceilings.

Until they ended up in the feasting hall, where an enormous fire crackled in the grate and a table was set for two by the leaping flames. Either side of the fireplace were tapestries and another wall was painted with a fabulous medieval mural.

'This is beautiful,' Amara said.

'It is. We really appreciate the effort you have put in,' Gio said.

'Then I will leave you both to it,' Claudette said.

Amara stood and took in the breakfast, different types of bread, cold meats, cheese, massive pretzels, honey and jam, along with a large steaming cafetière of coffee. 'This is amazing,' she said. And for a moment, a stupid moment, she wanted it to be real; that Gio had arranged this magical breakfast in a magical castle because magic existed. But it didn't and she mustn't forget that. This was a marriage of convenience. 'An excellent campaign stop,' she said lightly as she sat down. 'I'll take a photo.' As she pulled out her phone it pinged and instinctively, she looked down, saw the message and froze.

Hello, Amara. Lorenzo has sent a photograph of himself. I am sure you have already searched for him on social media, but just in case here it is. Nonno.

'Amara?' She heard Gio's concerned voice. 'Are you okay?'

'Yes.' She pushed down the wave of panic; right now, she didn't want to face reality. Wanted to lose herself in the illusion of the castle. Quickly she took a photo and then sat down. 'We'd better get started.'

On automatic she reached out and picked up

a piece of rye bread, a piece of cheese, a heart-shaped pretzel. Took a bite. Sipped the coffee.

'Amara? What's wrong?'

'Nothing. Why should anything be wrong?' Now she'd gone from over bright to over breezy. 'I'm fine.'

'Is this all a bit over the top? Fairy tale castle, romantic breakfast? I'm sorry I should have warned you.'

'No! This is lovely. And it's a great idea.' She managed to force her lips upwards. 'Sorry. I know I should be looking a bit more loved up in case someone comes in.'

'No!' Gio shook his head. 'That doesn't matter. What matters to me is that clearly something has upset you. I know it must have because you haven't said a single thing about the food.'

She glanced down at her plate and back up at him, suddenly absurdly touched that he'd even noticed, that he cared enough to ask. Neither Stefan nor Silvio had been so attuned to her moods, would have been relieved she'd not offered a running commentary.

'If you want to talk about it maybe I can help, but if you prefer to have a bit of space to think you definitely don't need to act any part.'

She looked across at him, saw nothing but

concern in his brown eyes and suddenly she did want to talk to him, all the feelings so raw, swirling round her brain. Maybe he could give her some perspective. After all he knew about Lorenzo and Daisy already.

'My grandfather has messaged me. About Lorenzo. My half-brother.' The words sounded wrong, alien, surreal and a sudden image of Luca flashed across her brain. Her real brother. Her twin. 'Lorenzo is planning to visit the Rossi estate in four days' time. He sent my grandfather a photograph.' Her voice caught and she gave an impatient shake of her head. 'I don't know why it hit me so badly. I mean I've known about Lorenzo for days now. I knew he was going to meet my grandfather.'

'But now it's real,' he said quietly.

'Exactly. I hadn't looked him up, or Daisy. Maybe because I don't want it to be real. And seeing him…it's set me in a spin. He looks like my father. Dark-haired, dark blue eyes. Same as my grandfather, as well. A true Rossi. Whereas I…'

'You are beautiful,' Gio said firmly. 'And you are a true Rossi.'

'Yes, but so is Lorenzo and…' She broke off. 'Just like you are a true Romano.' She stared at him, suddenly stricken, realising how terrible she must sound, as if she were doing to her half-brother what was done to Gio. Excluding him. 'I'm sorry. I shouldn't even be talking to you about this.'

'No. It's fine.' His voice was low and reassuring as he rose and moved round the table, shifted his chair closer to her. 'It's not comparable. Lorenzo has turned up out of the blue. You said he didn't even know who his father was until now. If your grandfather had known of his existence before, or if your father had acknowledged him, then everything may have been different. You would have grown up forming a bond. Now your feelings are natural. You're scared; you feel like your whole destiny is being threatened.' A shadow crossed his eyes and she wondered what he was thinking, wondered if he was thinking about his own half-brothers and how they would react to his arrival on the board.

'It is,' she said softly.

'Perhaps your destiny is being changed rather than threatened.'

'What's the difference?'

He thought for a moment. 'Your whole life you've known that you will run a vineyard. Haven't you ever wondered what you would have done if that wasn't your destiny? If you had a choice. If your destiny wasn't to continue your family's heritage?'

'No, I haven't. I always knew that was my life.' And that knowledge had been comforting, safe, secure. It defined her.

'Then perhaps you should think about it now,' he said gently. 'Face your biggest fear. You said yesterday that you may have to walk away from the estate for the sake of the estate. If that happened, what would you do?'

Her first instinct was to lash out, to tell him he didn't understand, couldn't understand and then she looked into his eyes, saw a seriousness there, a sympathy, but more than that she saw empathy and now she thought, really thought, about his apparent acceptance of what his family had done. They had given him acknowledgement without acceptance, he'd been forced to grow up in sight of the 'holy grail' of entry into the family business, but always knowing it was a prize that would be withheld. Had to endure being a second-class Romano; Gio had had to face that. 'Is that what you did?' she asked now.

'Yes.' His voice quiet now as if he were looking back into his past. 'When I was young, all I wanted was to be part of Romano Confectionery. I did everything I could think of to prove myself worthy.' And now she could picture the dark-haired young boy, desperate to please, trying to show his family that he deserved acceptance, was worthy of it and her heart twisted in sympathy. 'But in the end, I had to face it wasn't going to happen. That I was chasing an impossible dream and it was stopping me from finding anything else. I had to find my own path.'

'I'm sorry.'

He shook his head. 'I'm not. Because it gave me a chance to go and do something else, be myself, make my own destiny. I would never have discovered that I have a technological bent. I'd never have got the thrill and the satisfaction of founding my own company if I'd already had a future mapped out for me. And I do truly love my company. What I've achieved, what I hope to achieve. So maybe you should think about the possibility that good can come of forging your own path. An opportunity. To do something that is yours. As Amara not as a Rossi.'

And when she thought of all he'd achieved, thought about the real difference he'd made and was making, a small flicker of excitement ignited at the thought of the unknown. A flicker that flared and then died as she tried to think. 'I can't think of anything.'

'Don't sound so sad.' He reached out, took her hand in his and she felt the familiar jolt, but alongside something else. A warmth, a reassurance, a sense of being listened to, thought about. And she couldn't remember anyone other than Vittorio making her feel like that. And even with her grandfather, there was so much they didn't talk about, both of them intent on protecting the other. 'It's completely normal not to instantly think of another career path. And there's no rush.' He gave a sudden smile, and his brown eyes held a warmth that felt like a caress. 'I get that Lorenzo is coming in a few days, but he won't arrive in an armoured tank planning to take over the estate.'

The words held such understanding and Amara felt lighter, the bleak panic receding and she laid a hand on his forearm, revelled in the lithe muscle, the texture under her fingers. 'Thank you, Gio. For listening and giving me some perspective.' True perspective because to give it he'd had to share something of himself, of a childhood she sensed he didn't visit often and she valued that.

'That's okay. And I will be with you,' he said.

'What do you mean?'

'When Lorenzo comes to meet you, I will be there.'

A happiness touched her, along with a relief that she knew she had to clamp down on. Yet the idea of having support felt novel and beautiful and for a minute she wondered if it should alarm her. She shook the thought away. This was the beauty of this type of marriage. He wasn't coming out of duty or love because that wasn't what this was about. He was coming as part of their deal, to bolster the show. To demonstrate to her grandfather that she wouldn't be alone. That she could lead the Rossi estate. And that was a good, positive thing. She'd wanted support, a person, an extra body, and if she was glad on her own behalf, glad that it was *Gio* who would be there, she refused to acknowledge it.

'Thank you.' Reaching out she picked up the pretzel, layered on the cheese, and took a bite. 'This *is* lovely,' she said. 'I can taste the crunch of salt crystals and the cheese is incredibly nutty.'

She stopped as he laughed. 'Now I know you are feeling better,' he said. 'Because you're thinking about what you're eating. In fact… that's something else you could do. You could be a food critic; come to that, you could be a wine critic. You could research and write books, travel the world.'

Amara looked at him, imagined a completely different life, a life where she travelled, wrote about wine, about food, experimented with cooking, did a Cordon Bleu course. She and Gio could go to… She stopped the thought. She and Gio—there was no Amara and Gio. They were going to live separate lives. Do their own thing. The last thing Gio would want to do was accompany her everywhere, be at her beck and call. They were going to walk alone, coming together sometimes when circumstances demanded it. And that was what she wanted. Her space and solitude, control. Not being close to anyone. Because that's when things got complicated. 'I'll bear it in mind,' she said. 'And I'll start by trying this pastry right here.'

'Good plan. And when we're finished, we can look round the castle and then head for our next destination.'

# CHAPTER EIGHT

TWO HOURS LATER, Gio pulled into a parking space. 'I thought we'd break the journey here. It's meant to be a truly picturesque little Bavarian village.'

And as they walked through the cobbled streets of the old town he couldn't help but agree with the reviews. The houses and shops, which dated back to the fourteenth century, had kept all their medieval charm. In addition, the pastel façades were made unique by the paintings that adorned them, biblical references as well as scenes of everyday life in such detail that they kept stopping to study them. The whole made all the more awe-inspiring by the backdrop of the Alps that loomed up and overlooked the town.

'Another magical place,' Amara said. 'Another fairy tale setting. Good thing I know fairy tales are just a story,' she said. 'There are no glass slippers or hundred-year sleeps.

And kisses do not turn frogs into handsome princes.'

'No,' he agreed. 'But let's not rule kisses out completely. I think they have a part to play in marriage. And kisses can be pretty magical in any setting.'

Pink tinged her cheeks and he wondered if she was remembering the kisses they'd shared, or waking up that morning accidentally entwined in each other arms. The memory caused a sudden rush; her nearness, the soft welcoming warmth of her, her hand on his chest, her fingers over the beat of his heart, her hair tickling his chest.

Gio took a deep breath, decided it would be a good idea to change the subject, before he offered to demonstrate how magical a kiss could be right here and now. 'There's apparently an amazing Baroque church that's worth a visit—if you'd like to see it.'

'Sounds good.' As they walked down the cobbled street, lined with small stores and cafés, she glanced up at him. 'Have you been to Bavaria before?' she asked. 'You seem to know your way around.'

He shook his head. 'No. This plan is all down to some internet searches and trying to come up with a few places that fit our story.' Even as he said the words he knew they weren't strictly true; he'd been looking for places that Amara might enjoy, as well. He'd known that it must have been exhausting playing to the audience the previous night in a celebrity-studded place under scrutiny, and had wanted today to be more laid-back. 'I wanted to at least try to make this a bit of a holiday. Have *you* been to Bavaria before?' he asked. 'Is that why you chose to come here to think?'

She shook her head. 'It was a fairly random selection. I thought the cold might clear my brain.'

They arrived at the church and halted, stood and absorbed its beauty, the soaring rise of the bell tower, the painted frescoes of St Peter and St Paul.

'It's incredible really to think of how many people have stood here, how many people over the centuries have gone inside to worship or pray or perhaps simply for a sense of peace,' she said softly.

'Shall we go in?'

She nodded and they stepped forward into the incredible interior, the whole place surprisingly light thanks to the massive arched windows. Amara craned her neck to study the ceiling painting and he followed suit, took in the story of the saints, then turned his attention to the red marble of the altar, the numerous Baroque paintings, the statues and gilded, golden pieces and the overall sense of awe and majesty.

'So full of so much beauty,' she said softly

He nodded and took her hand in his, wanted her to know he shared her sense of awe and appreciation until a few minutes later, by tacit consent, they left and headed back into the crisp, cold air.

'Café?' he suggested and they moved towards one of the many picturesque eateries that lined the cobbled streets. Once inside they sat at one of the wooden tables, covered in a red-patterned cloth and ordered coffee.

'So, you came somewhere cold to think? Where would you usually go on holiday?'

'I don't really travel much or if I do, it's work-related. The vineyard is hard work and neither my grandfather nor I are very good at delegation. Growing up we didn't really go on holiday much—I think my grandfather felt awkward taking me on holiday on my own. He is pretty fit for his age, but he couldn't run around after me. And child-friendly holidays weren't really his thing. He would sometimes go away with one of his…relationships, but he didn't take me. He didn't really like involving any of his girlfriends in my upbringing. He said it wasn't fair.

For either party to get attached.' She shook her head. 'Some of them tried though, but I wasn't having any of it. I was happy with it just being my grandfather and me.'

Gio studied her face, tried to imagine her childhood, wondered how old she'd been when she'd lost her parents. He could have tried to find out, though he wasn't sure how easy it would be with the information he had, but he had elected to not even try. If Amara wanted to share her past she would.

Her expression turned sad. 'I thought he was happy too. But now I wonder if he always wished for a larger family, if maybe he didn't remarry because of me. And I also wonder if he wants great-grandchildren so he can enjoy them without the responsibility of being a surrogate parent.' She stilled, her hand hovering over her plate. 'Actually, that's something we haven't even spoken about. Children.'

For an instant an image flashed through Gio's mind, himself and Amara and next to them were two children, a boy and a girl. He blinked fiercely to dispel the images. The idea too much, too enormous to contemplate as a reality. An idea that wouldn't work, couldn't work within this arrangement. And that was fine with him. Of course it was.

'You're right,' he said. 'We haven't and we should.'

'You go first,' she said and he saw a wariness in her tone, in her green eyes.

'I've always believed I wouldn't have children. I never intended to have a long-term relationship so it wasn't something I ever considered as a possibility.' And that had been a relief. Because he wasn't sure he could be a good parent. Maybe never experiencing good parenting meant you couldn't be a good parent yourself. Couldn't manage the responsibility even if he was pretty damn sure he knew what that responsibility entailed—it meant making your child your priority, being present, spending time with them. Making sure they knew they were loved and *wanted.*

'And now?'

'Now…given the type of arrangement we have agreed on, I still don't think it is possible. But I'd like to hear your thoughts.' Now wariness touched him; from everything Amara had said the future of the Rossi estate was of paramount importance to her. Vittorio Rossi wanted heirs. Amara was faced with watching her half-siblings provide heirs, with the possibility of being pushed out from the future of the estate. 'What about you?'

She picked up the coffee, put it down again. 'I used to think I would have children. But after Stefan, after Silvio, I knew I wouldn't. But when I think about it, it makes me feel guilty because I know how happy it would make my grandfather but…'

'Would it make you happy?' he asked. 'You shouldn't have a child to make someone else happy.'

'We're getting married to make other people happy.'

'And that's our decision to make. It impacts us. And I wouldn't do it if it was going to make either of us unhappy. But either way it is our choice. Children don't ask to be born.' He could hear the edge to his tone, he knew what it felt like not to be wanted. His mother was at best ambivalent and his father would have happily erased him from the timeline. 'And I should make something very clear. I won't be used to provide the Rossi heir. If I have a child, I want to be part of that child's life. Properly. I won't be a part-time dad.'

Now anger flashed from her eyes as she pushed her cup aside in a jerky gesture. 'If you think I would ever stoop so low as to use you for a child then I suggest we call this whole marriage off. Right here, right now. Do you believe I'd do that to you? Do that to a child. To a baby. Bring them into the world if I didn't want them, just to make my grandfather happy?'

He closed his eyes at the sheer outrage in her voice. 'No, I don't think that,' he said quietly. 'But that's not enough. I have to be sure. How can I not be? That would be wrong. I know what it's like to be a child who isn't wanted, to be shunted around at other people's whims. I won't let that or any echo of that happen to my child.' He paused for breath, wondered how this situation had got so out of hand. He couldn't remember the last time he'd had such a heated discussion with anyone, the last time he'd cared enough about something to argue. Now in the heat of the moment he'd shared something he hadn't meant to. But it had needed to be said. He wanted Amara to understand that he meant what he said, that it was important. And he didn't regret it.

There was a silence and then, to his surprise, she reached out, touched his arm, left it there. 'I'm sorry. You're right. You can't know for sure my motivations on a few days' notice. But I agree with you. I don't want to bring children into our marriage. I know children aren't for me and our arrangement doesn't change that. But for what it's worth, in an alternate universe if I were ever to be a mum I would want my child, and I would love that child and do my best to give my child a happy childhood.' And there was that image again. Of Amara holding a baby, *their* baby, with him by her side. But she was right; that was a different universe, another timeline. He heard sincerity in her voice but he heard sadness too. Then she reached out, covered his hand with hers. 'And I'm sorry that your childhood wasn't how I imagined it to be.'

'How did you imagine it?' Perhaps he should close the conversation down, but he didn't want to. He wanted Amara to understand that what he'd said had come from his heart, that he hadn't been trying to shoot her down or accuse her.

'I suppose I assumed you had quite a laid-back privileged rock 'n' roll childhood with your mum. I know you aren't close with your dad, but I assumed that meant you didn't see him very often.' She shook her head. 'That's a lot of assuming. I'm sorry.'

'You don't have to apologise.'

'So how was it in reality?'

'My mum and I—we get on okay now, but when I was young she wasn't very present. She was never cruel to me, or deliberately unkind, she just didn't really have any interest in me. She never wanted children—she's always been honest about that. So somehow, she felt that excused her from having to be at all maternal.

It was more as though I was a stray dog who she had taken in during a moment of charity and now wasn't quite sure what to do with. So, she handed me over to her entourage and got on with living her life exactly as if she didn't have a child. It was a bit like sending the dog to a kennel I suppose.'

He tried to keep his voice amused, light, but he had the feeling he wasn't fooling Amara, and tried to hide it with facts.

'The problem was that her entourage weren't interested in me or babysitting me. They were there because they adored my mother. I mean I do understand I probably wasn't much of a draw compared to a rock 'n' roll lifestyle, so I was definitely the short straw. It was great for building self-reliance and I became a dab hand at making sure they didn't misplace me, but it wasn't the sort of upbringing I would want for my child. I would want to be there, present, part of my child's life.' He shrugged. 'That's why I got so heated. I didn't mean to accuse you.'

'I understand that.' Her voice was soft, all her previous anger gone. 'Thank you for telling me and I am sorry that your mum was like that. Sorry for you, but I am also sorry for her.' He saw the anger in her eyes, an anger he knew was directed at his mother, but he saw no hint of the pity he dreaded so much.

'I don't think many people feel sorry for my mother,' he said, still trying to keep it light.

But Amara was having none of it. 'Well, I do,' she said roundly. 'Because she missed out on you, watching you grow, spending time with you, seeing you become the kind, caring, successful man you have become. She could have been part of that journey and she missed out. Big time. And no amount of hit songs or concerts or wild parties can make up for that. She missed out and that is not your fault. You are not a short straw and it is on her if she believed that.'

He forced his expression to remain still, touched by her words but aware that Amara didn't know the whole of it. It wasn't only his mother who had seen him as a short straw, it had been his father, as well. And Gio knew that was personal, knew his father loathed the sight of him. Salvatore Romano was a family man, with a wife, and two other sons he had always treated well. Gio could excuse his mother, she'd never wanted a child full stop. But his father as well? It seemed to him the common denominator was Gio himself.

The passion in Amara's voice, the caring, warmed him but made him feel edgy at the same time. Conversations like this brought closeness and sharing and those were all things to be wary of. ‘Thank you,’ he said. ‘Truly. But now how about we try a piece of cake?’

‘Works for me,’ she said and he was grateful that she seemed to instinctively understand the need to back off, the abrupt change of subject. ‘I’d love to try the *Prinzregententorte* if they have any. I read about it somewhere. It’s really thin layers of sponge filled with buttercream and then covered in chocolate.’

‘Sounds good.’ He eyed her. ‘Is there anything else you’d like to try? I’m happy to let you choose for me.’

She grinned at him. ‘How well you know me!’ There was a sudden silence as if they were each realising both the truth of the statement and its absurdity. After all, he’d only met Amara two days before. ‘I’d love to try the apple torte if that’s okay with you.’

‘No problem at all.’

And as they shared the two cakes, discussed the merits of different fruit fillings, how it was possible to make such a light sponge, the texture of different creams, Gio was aware of a sense of contentment, told himself it was okay to enjoy it. This period of time with Amara was important, crucial to setting up this whole marriage. It had to look real and they had to spend time together. Soon enough they would announce the engagement and then the proverbial would hit the fan when his father found out what was going down. But there wouldn't be a damn thing he could do about it. And that was what was most important. And that was what this marriage was about. Once the actual wedding took place, once he was safely on the board, it would be different. Everything would change. Amara would be caught up with the Rossi estate and forging a relationship with her siblings and he would be caught up in all the flak and difficulties of combatting his father. This was a period of respite for them both. Nothing more.

It was dark when they reached the chalet they were staying in for the night. 'Here we are,' she said and they both peered out. Amara gave a sigh of mingled relief and satisfaction; she'd chosen the chalet based on the fairy tale whirlwind romance theme and it looked like she'd made a good choice.

'How lovely. They've put the lights on for us. I'm guessing they're on a timer.'

The chalet glowed like a beacon, illuminating the wooden building in a yellow gold aura;

swirls of snow fell on the twinkling lights that adorned the snow-dusted sloping gables of the roof.

'It's perfect,' he said. 'So now I suggest we grab our bags and make a run for it.'

They did exactly that, through the swirls of snow that flurried down from the starry skies, each flake landing with a sizzle on her face as she put the code into the key safe and retrieved the key.

The interior was beautiful, yet another fairy tale image and she was beginning to think she should just cave in and live in the fairy tale for a few days. Allow herself to believe all of this was real whilst knowing it was fake.

The idea whirled through her mind and she tried to imagine what they would do if they were a real couple. Imagined walking hand in hand through the property, imagined… Enough.

'Shall we look round?' he asked and she nodded. As they walked through the rooms she took in the rustic cosiness of the décor, the warm lighting shining from lamps ensconced in the wood-panelled wall enclosures, comfortable, brightly coloured sofas and armchairs arranged round a massive fireplace, loaded with the sweet-smelling scent of freshly cut logs.

The kitchen housed a range cooker and a polished wooden table. Amara checked her phone. 'I asked them to leave us a dinner we could heat up, unless you'd rather eat out. I thought if we stay in, we can take photos and big up the "romance" of a cosy night in by the fireplace.' She gave a sudden gurgle of laughter. 'Unless you think that's a bit over the top and completely out of character for Gio Romano.'

'But remember I am a reformed, new Gio Romano, caught up in a whirlwind romance. I am pretty sure I can come up with some believable moves in my new persona.'

Amara couldn't help herself. 'What sort of moves?' she asked softly.

'Well,' he said and now he moved a little closer to her. 'I'd put dinner onto a slow heat and then whilst it was cooking, I'd suggest… various ways we could work up an appetite.'

Amara gulped, managed a smile. She wasn't going to let this attraction take over, even as she realised she had taken a step closer to him. 'Good idea,' she said. 'We could…go for a brisk run in the snow.'

'We could. Followed by a slow session in the sauna.' For an instant Amara imagined Gio, chest bare, sat in the sauna, herself next to him, both of them warm and glowing and close and… She blinked, took a determined step away from him and headed to the fridge, tempted to stick her head in it in an attempt to cool her thoughts down. Carefully she took the casserole dish out and lifted the lid, looked at the contents, relieved to have a new topic of conversation.

'It says here this is Flädlesuppe, which is a pancake soup to start with. Sliced pancakes which look a bit like noodles in a clear broth. Followed by another more filling soup called Brotsuppe.'

'Bread soup?' he asked.

'Yup.' She opened the second dish. 'But I think it's a posh, luxury version.' She inhaled. 'There are definitely some aromatic spices in there and I'm pretty sure I can smell caraway and nutmeg. And after the soup they've put together a picnic dinner. I'll start heating the soups up.' Somehow it seemed important to keep talking, to try and forget the idea of steamy saunas and Gio's moves. Keep focused.

Once the food was heating, Amara scrolled down her phone. 'I thought I'd check to see how we're doing publicity wise,' she said. 'And it looks good. I guess we should think about what we do next. How we escalate to make the engagement believable. To the public but also to my grandfather.' As she said the words, anxiety emerged as she tried to imagine telling Vittorio that she was engaged, that she and Gio were in love. Realised the enormity of the lie, the enormity of what they were doing.

'You're worried about telling him?' The words half question, half statement. 'Do you think he'll disapprove of us getting married so fast? Or will he disapprove of me because of my dating history?'

'Some or all of the above. But mostly I'm worried because I want him to believe it's real, that I've found love. But I don't think I've ever lied to him about something important. And love is important to him. He wouldn't want me to marry without it. I don't think your reputation or the timing will matter to him as long as he believes we love each other. So half of me is scared we won't be able to pull it off and the other half hates lying to him.'

'I get that.' He turned to face her, his back against the worktop so she could see his expression. 'I don't like lying either, but I am not sure what we will achieve by telling him the truth. He wants you to be happy. I hope our marriage will make you happy.'

'I think it will,' she said. 'I really do.' And stood there right now she was sure of it, mesmerised by his sheer presence, by the sincerity of his intent. And she had an urge to reach out to gently cradle his face in her hands, to move closer to him. *Whoa, Amara.* That was attraction speaking. She wasn't marrying him just so she could go to bed with him. She was marrying him because it made sense. Would make her grandfather happy. 'I guess the only option is to lie.' Because there was no love in this marriage and for an insensible fleeting moment that made her feel sad. A sadness she pushed away. Love begat sadness. She looked at him, willed him to understand as they carried the soup over to the table. 'But I don't think he'd understand our arrangement and he would hate the idea I was marrying without love. Or doing this for him in any way.' They sat and started to eat, and she took a few minutes to savour the taste. 'So somehow, I have to pull this off when I tell him. All these years he's been there for me, changed his entire life for me. It took Lorenzo and Daisy's arrival to show me how hard it has been for him. How hard I have made it for him.' She bit her lip, turned her head away as she felt tears coming.

'No. Amara, I don't think it was like that. I think your grandfather loves you and he wants you to be happy. I think you have both been through so much that I don't know about, but he stepped up for you and that was the right thing to do. I am sure you brought him so much joy over the years.'

'Not enough. Without him…' Her voice caught and something twisted in his chest. 'I couldn't have survived without him. Quite literally really. He brought me up.' She looked across the table at him. 'After the accident.'

'You don't have to talk about it if you don't want to,' he said softly. 'I don't know what happened and I haven't tried to find out.'

The fact that he hadn't checked up, hadn't tried to work out what had happened, had decided to let her share her past if and when she was ready, warmed her and she knew that she wanted him to understand, to really know why this was so important to her. 'I'd like to tell you.'

'Why don't we move into the lounge? We can eat the next course later?' She nodded. 'I'll light a fire and we can talk.'

# CHAPTER NINE

ONCE AGAIN AMARA appreciated what Gio was doing; giving her a chance to make sure she really did want to do this. Wanted to discuss something painful and personal. But he also wanted her to be able to do it in a place where she would feel comfortable, and his thoughtfulness touched her. Curled up on an oversized sofa, she watched him prepare the fire, saw the sparks light and flare into crackling reddish-orange flames and she knew she did want to tell him. Wanted him to understand the depth of her motivation, her love for her grandfather. Wanted to share a little of her life just as he had shared a little of his earlier in the day. She marshalled her thoughts.

'My family died in a helicopter accident. I was the only survivor. If I had been sitting in a different seat, I guess I would have died too. Instead, somehow, I got thrown clear of the wreckage—I broke my arm and a rib but otherwise I was fine. I woke up in the hospital and for a few minutes I thought it was all going to be okay and then I knew inside me that it wasn't. Something told me that I'd lost a connection I'd had all my life. With my brother, my twin.' Gio stilled. 'He died too. Luca. My twin brother.'

'Oh, Amara.' In one seamless move he shifted toward her and then she was in his arms, held close, the warmth of his body so full of comfort that she could feel tears start to form and she blinked fiercely.

'Hey. It's okay to cry. I wish I knew what to say, but all I can say is that I am truly sorry. How old were you both?'

'Four,' she said softly and felt his arms tighten around her.

'I can't imagine how it must have felt having that bond severed.'

'It was like I had lost a part of me. A part of my soul. A part of my being that can't ever be replaced. I remember opening my eyes and feeling a void. Then I was looking round for my parents and they weren't there. Then my grandfather came in and he looked… Broken. Like a ghost. He told me that my parents were gone and my grandmother. And Luca. It felt as if my world shattered. My world did shatter. It was all gone. And I felt alone in a way I never had before.'

'Tell me about Luca.' Gio's voice was soft.

'We were very, very close. I knew what he was thinking and he knew the same for me. We fought sometimes, of course we did, but we truly were best friends. Luca was naughtier than me—he'd always come up with some plan. To sneak an extra cookie or stay awake a little longer. And he'd always persuade me to go along with it. To help.'

She could hear the smile in Gio's voice. 'I bet even at that age you improved the plan.'

'I did! I've always thought that if he'd lived, he and I would have made a perfect team. I can imagine him coming up with the idea to make a wine that would be really out there and me working out a way to actually do it and the wine being amazing. Even when we were kids, we kind of sparked off each other, we were a team. After the accident, I knew nothing could ever be the same again—I'd never have that kind of bond again. Losing it was like severing something vital in me. It changed me somehow.' It had numbed her, deadened something inside her. Had killed off her ability to love anyone new. She still loved her grandfather because she'd already loved him. She still loved her family even though they didn't walk this earth any more. But she knew there was something broken inside her, which was why she couldn't have a loving relationship, couldn't risk having children, couldn't risk new bonds when she knew the pain of losing them. But she was good with that, because her inability to love kept her safe. Instinctively she shifted a little closer to Gio, and a sudden qualm struck her, one she pushed away. After all she *was* safe, protected, behind her wall, her barriers that didn't really let anyone close. Not in ways it counted.

'When you compound that with the loss of your parents as well, that must have been earth-shattering,' he said slowly. 'I am so sorry. And now the fact these new siblings are twins must be wrenching you.'

Amara nodded. 'What are the chances of two half-siblings you had no knowledge of suddenly turning up out of the blue and upending everything you believed? It's not just the fact they are twins that is wrenching. Their sheer existence overturns everything I believed to be true. They've rewritten my past.'

'Shattered your world all over again,' he said and she paused, arrested by the sheer understanding embodied, encapsuled, in those words.

'Yes. My favourite photo has always been a picture of my parents and Luca and me. Taken on the vineyard—a happy family. It was taken a month or so before the accident. But now that photo…it feels fake, false. The story I've always believed, that my parents loved each other—it turns out that it *is* a story, a *fictional* fairy tale.' Another reason, if she needed one, why she and Gio could never have children. Because it would be fake—what would she tell them? *Your mama and papa got married as part of an arrangement. We live separate lives but we both love you. We just don't believe in loving each other.* Or would they lie? Create another fictional fairy tale. She couldn't do that. 'None of what I believed is true. My father was married when he slept with Lorenzo and Daisy's mother. And then he walked away.' Had he loved her? Presumably not. 'That means nothing is how I thought it was and I'll never know the answers. I'll never know the truth and I can no longer take comfort from the past.'

'It must seem as though you have lost them all over again.'

Gio really got it and she moved closer to him, felt the reassurance of his bulk next to her.

'I get that,' he said softly. 'I do. And I understand that you must be wishing Lorenzo and Daisy had never shown up. That you could keep the story, that it was true.'

His arm was around her now and she was nestled close, the sensation unfamiliar and yet strangely comfortable, as his words further demonstrated his understanding of how she felt.

'But...' He hesitated and she gestured with her hand.

'It's okay. Please share your thoughts. I value them.'

'Okay.' He thought for a moment, clearly wanting to choose his words carefully. 'You're right, you may never know the full truth of this, all of this, but none of it is Lorenzo and Daisy's fault.'

'I know that. But I also know they are gaining so much—a wonderful grandfather and a heritage that...'

'That maybe they don't want.' His voice was gentle. 'I understand all that you have lost and the pain it must be causing you. But they have lost something too. They have spent their whole lives believing they have a different father, believed that they shared blood and genetics and a heritage with the man who brought them up.'

Amara gave a small gasp as the knowledge slammed into her. 'You're right,' she said, heard the smallness of her voice. 'All I've been thinking of is myself and my feelings and that's not fair or right. It's selfish.'

Instinctively she tried to move away from him, but he still held her close. 'No. It's not. That's not what I meant at all. It's completely normal for you to feel exactly how you are feeling. And…it could be that Lorenzo and Daisy are terrible people. I am not advocating that you fall on them with happiness, I mean…'

'That maybe they are struggling too.'

'Maybe,' he said. 'But that doesn't take away from how you are feeling or make those feelings any less valid. But don't be too hard on them or yourself. Or your father.'

'What he did was wrong. I have always believed he was perfect.'

'Of course you have. You lost him when you were so young. What he did was wrong—I can't try and excuse that. But although what he did was inexcusable it doesn't mean that he was all bad. It doesn't define the whole of him. It doesn't mean that the photo that you love doesn't hold truth. I believe it does. What he did doesn't mean he didn't love you and Luca. Doesn't mean your mother didn't love you both. Think back to your memories of them. With you. What are they like?'

Amara thought back, felt her face break into a smile. 'I remember laughter, and I remember my dad throwing us up in the air, telling me I could reach the sky and I remember stretching my fingers up to the clouds. I remember my mum brushing my hair and telling me stories. I remember my dad baking with me, all of us making a birthday cake. And he got me to smell all the different things, the cinnamon and the vanilla and the sugar, even the milk. My mum playing hide-and-seek with us.'

'Then no matter what *their* relationship was, they both loved you and that is incredibly precious. Don't let what has happened tarnish or taint your memories of that. That photo is the truth—that was a real happy moment and you should treasure it.'

The intensity, the gravity of his words, was palpable and she knew they came from a place of truth. Knew too that Gio didn't have any of those memories; his mother hadn't played with him, or held his hand, hadn't been there for him. His father had acknowledged him, but that seemed to be pretty much it.

'Thank you,' she said softly. 'Truly. Everything you have said has made a massive difference to me.' She turned to face him.

And he was so close, so close she could see the length of his eyelashes, the glint of firelight dappling his skin. She could see the compassion and the intentness in his brown eyes and she could see that intent morph from compassion to a different type of intent.

Saw latent desire spark into reality, saw his pupils darken, his jaw clench and felt him start to move away.

And she knew that she didn't want him to. Didn't want to move away either. Didn't want to do anything but this and so she moved forward and brushed her lips against his, an invitation and a question.

Then he was kissing her, really kissing her and this kiss was off the scale, completely different from their previous kisses. There was no doubt now and sensing that, Amara too surrendered to desire, freely and willingly, not even a vestige of reservation in her mind. She wanted this, wanted him, her whole body crying out in need.

Then she stopped thinking, lost herself completely in a kiss so sensual, so overpowering, so glorious. Desire swirled as he deepened the kiss and now she was pressed so close to him, so very close, but it wasn't close enough. She needed to feel his body against hers and now she was fumbling with his shirt, pulling at the buttons and for one awful second he broke the kiss.

But the loss was only fleeting as he rose and gathered her up to lay her down on the sheepskin rug in front of the flicker and flare of the fire. And then he was unzipping her dress, his fingers lingering on her skin, on her body, teasing, tantalising. She pulled his shirt off, revelling in the feel of his shoulders under her fingers, watching the glow of the flames dapple the muscle and breadth of him and then he was lying next to her, kissing her, touching her and she relished touching and being touched, lost in a vortex of pleasure.

Gio half opened his eyes, instantly aware that something was missing. Not something. Someone. Amara. In the moment between sleep and waking he felt a smile curve his lips as he recalled the previous night, let the memories wash over him. The sheer joy, elation, pleasure given and received. The soft sound of her laughter, the intensity of her reactions, her generosity and her passion. The taste of her, the tickle of her hair, the flecks of emerald pleasure in the depth of her eyes. Recalled picking her up and carrying her to the bedroom, the renewed passion, the wonder and the awe as they continued to learn and explore each other, until finally sated they'd fallen asleep, still entwined.

But now he frowned slightly. Where was she? He reached out, felt the warmth of the bedsheets and now he opened his eyes fully and turned, saw Amara perched on the end of the bed, carefully edging away.

'Morning,' he said softly and she jumped slightly, before turning to look at him, her glorious red hair tumbling past her bare shoulders, the edge of the duvet pulled up.

'Morning,' she said and he saw a wariness in her eyes. 'I was going to go and sort out breakfast and tidy up. I'm sorry I didn't want to wake you up…' the words were coming out in a breathless tumble and she was continuing to edge away.

Carefully he held on to the duvet, his mind racing. Last night Amara had shared so much, given so much. Spoken about her family, her twin, the raw pain of loss and grief, she'd revisited memories, shared something precious with him. And then attraction had overwhelmed them. They'd slept together without discussion, or planning or thought. So right now, she must be feeling vulnerable and all he wanted to do was reassure her. Even as a small warning bell tolled at the back of his own brain, telling him that perhaps Amara was right to be wary.

But now the most important thing was to reassure her. 'Amara?'

'Yes.'

'Why don't you come back to bed?' He smiled at her. 'Unless this is a cunning plan to pull the duvet off me. You don't need a plan. You just need to ask.'

Now she blushed and he saw a small smile begin to upturn her lips.

He patted the space next to him.

'Come on—come back to bed. Talk to me.'

She hesitated and then scooted back so she was sat next to him, both of them propped against the headboard, though he noticed the tension in her body, the scrupulous care she took not to let their bodies touch.

'What's wrong?' he asked. 'Are you regretting last night?' He glanced at her and decided that the direct approach was best. 'Because I'm not. I'm glad. I'm honoured you told me about Luca, about your parents.'

Amara turned to him. 'Truly?' she asked. 'You see, I never talk about Luca or my family. It's too raw, too painful, something I hold close to myself.'

'It's also something precious and I feel privileged that you shared your memories with me.'

'Thank you, Gio.'

Her smile was small but genuine, and admiration surged inside him at the inner strength she must have to negotiate so much pain and loss. Well, she no longer had to navigate that alone. The thought stopped him in his tracks. *Whoa. Hold your horses, Gio.* Their whole marriage was about wanting to be alone. About not living in each other's pockets. About not being answerable to each other or responsible for the other's happiness.

He pushed the thought away, told himself there was nothing wrong with being supportive, nothing wrong with caring.

'And as for what happened later, it's not possible for me to regret that.' They were on safer ground here and he risked a smile. 'Turns out we are super compatible, Richter scale compatible.' Now sudden uncharacteristic doubt touched him. 'Or at least that's how I see it. If I've got it wrong then…'

'Well actually… Given that we are faking a whole whirlwind romance I thought it would be best to…' Then seeing his expression her impish smile broke out. 'You haven't got it wrong,' she said softly. 'Last night was… I haven't really got words. It was magical, the kind of thing you do read about but don't believe really exists.' She broke off. 'It was definitely great sex.'

Gio recalled their words of the previous days, the idea that they would be compatible. Well that was a definite—Amara was right—they had definitely shared great sex. Yet the thoughts that streamed through his brain were of holding her, the way she'd nestled into his body, a desire to keep his arm around her to keep her safe. Enough. That was just the aftermath of great sex. A chemistry, a physical connection that they had already known they had. A physical connection that had nothing to do with emotion. Physics, chemistry, great sex. 'It was,' he said. 'I know we were planning on waiting, but I'm good with what happened. I hope you are too.'

'I'm good with it too,' she said, but he heard a soupçon of doubt in her voice and as if to echo that she shifted a little away from him before turning. 'Right. I'm ravenous. Breakfast and then we should make a plan for the day.' Now she moved further away and he sensed the conversation was over. 'Maybe we could have the picnic supper as a picnic breakfast?'

'Great plan.'

Twenty minutes later they reconvened and he noticed she'd set the table in the kitchen, clearly had no wish to return to the lounge and he wasn't sure he could blame her. Knew it was important for them both to remember, in the here and now, that the most important thing was the campaign trail.

'This all looks great,' he said as she laid out bread and cold meats and cheese.

As they started to eat, she looked across at him. 'So what's today's plan?'

'I thought we could go and visit a vineyard. You said you wanted to do that at our first dinner so why not today? I don't want you to miss out on one of the reasons you came here.' And maybe it would ground Amara, give her back some normality when everything felt overwhelming and when he could sense her vulnerability. From the emotions of the night before, from shared intimacy. 'Maybe even stay somewhere nearby so you can maximise your time there.'

Now he was rewarded by a massive smile. 'Really? Are you sure? I mean, won't it be boring for you?'

'Absolutely not. In fact, I've been doing some research and I'm genuinely interested—I hadn't realised there was so much cutting-edge technology associated with wine. It's fascinating, especially the AI tech.'

'It's a difficult balance.' She spread butter on a piece of bread and then added cheese and salami. 'Between tradition and new ways, I don't think I could ever completely back AI over human instinct, knowledge and experience, but I know technology cannot be ignored. Not if you want to continue to thrive in today's world. But I would hate it to become that any grape could be controlled to grow anywhere, until there are uniform vineyards throughout the globe.'

He nodded. 'I don't think AI can replace your love for the wine you are creating. Or your human instinct.'

'I'm guessing the same goes for chocolate,' she said thoughtfully. 'Though nowadays there is so much mass-produced stuff.'

'That is what my grandparents don't agree with. I mean, they accept that products have to be produced in bulk, but it is really important to them to keep it as close to the original handmade chocolate as possible.'

'How did it all start?' Amara asked.

'It all started out small,' he said. 'I suppose like once upon a time the Rossi estate only grew a few vines and produced a few bottles of wine. Romano's started out as a small bakery run by my great-grandfather. He and my great-grandmother expanded into larger premises and then opened up a number of bakeries in neighbouring towns and villages. All family run. My grandfather was at the counter at the main store one day when my grandmother came in.' It was a story Aurelio was fond of telling, a story that Gio could somehow picture as he told it to Amara. His grandmother dressed in a chic tailored skirt and blouse, perfectly groomed. His grandfather a young man, dressed for work in an apron. 'She'd brought some of her homemade chocolate and wanted to know if the bakery would sell it on her behalf. My grandfather said he fell in love with her and her chocolate at the same moment. And that's where it started. Soon the bakery became known for the chocolate. My grandmother said love made her improve her recipe—that love was the magic ingredient.'

He glanced at Amara, wondered if she'd scoff but she didn't. Her face was intent as she listened and he remembered that she'd said that Vittorio Rossi had loved his wife, as well. And for a moment, Gio wished that somehow love was possible for him even as he knew it wasn't. Knew he wasn't capable of loving or being loved. Knew he wouldn't be enough, that there was something flawed inside him. That something that his grandparents had taken for granted was something that he couldn't understand. Like some people understood equations and others didn't.

'Go on,' she said.

'Well after they got married, Aurelio and Ava decided to branch out, to set up a separate confectioner's and then as time went on, they slowly expanded, grew the business. A business based on the premise of quality. That is their guiding principle. Romano chocolate is the real thing, not processed rubbish that shouldn't even be allowed to be marketed as chocolate. They want to preserve the ethos behind what they started. Chocolate that is a treat, something to be savoured and enjoyed. They would never produce or align themselves with a company that markets massive bars of cheap, badly made chocolate.'

'And that's what your father wants to do?'

'Yes. He claims that it isn't possible to retain my grandfather's principles and survive.'

Gio heard his voice harden. 'I disagree. My grandparents have managed the company with incredible success for the past fifty years and

I respect their principles and I believe they are right. Romano Confectionery is known for its quality. Its chocolate is the real thing. I understand that the profit margins matter, but not at the expense of quality. I believe in moving forward, in research and development, in trying to find ways to keep quality without sacrificing price. As a private company it should be possible to have profit margins that are acceptable to us personally rather than being accountable to the stock market.'

'You do really care,' Amara said softly.

'Yes, I do,' he said. He couldn't help it. 'Maybe it is in my blood. Or maybe it is because I know how much my grandparents have put into the company, how hard they have worked, how important it is.' Or maybe it was the fact that admission to the family business had always been the prize he thought he could never have, would never be good enough, worthy enough to win. Maybe he cared because this ultimate prize was finally within his grasp. Now his grandparents did see him as a true Romano. But did they? Or was this simply a move they had made of necessity? A temporary solution. A means to bring his father to heel and then they'd let Gio go. The thoughts caused a swirl of emotion and for a minute he questioned his decision to walk back into the family fold. Back into the conflicting complexities of a relationship he didn't really understand. Gio shook his head. 'My grandparents built the company up—they deserve to have their vision followed.' That was what was at stake.

'My grandfather says the earth, the land, the grapes belong to all the generations, but it is the responsibility of each generation to respect those gone past and those to come. I guess it's the same idea.'

Gio nodded. 'Those are very wise words,' he said. 'And if I can I intend to make sure that principle is honoured.' It was a good principle and he felt determination retrigger inside him. He would make this happen, would make sure Romano Confectionery thrived. And to do that he needed to be married. A plan began to form in his head, a plan that caused a flutter of anticipation in his gut, a thrill that he told himself was simple satisfaction at the idea of progress. Was nothing to do with Amara at all.

'We'd better get up and get going. I just need to make some calls.'

A few hours later they arrived at the vineyard and Gio turned to Amara, kept his voice casual. 'Looking forward to this?' he asked.

'Absolutely. I spoke to Erika Merz, her family have owned the vineyard for the past three generations and she sounds wonderful. In fact, from what she said the whole family sounds wonderful and we have so much to talk about. They've recently started making a red wine, having only made white wines, and we're starting with a tour of the vineyard.' She hesitated. 'Are you going to come for that?'

'I wish I could, but I've got some work calls and meetings I have to take.' This was true, but he had other plans as well, needed some time to implement them.

Yet he was aware of a wish to stay with Amara. To watch her in her element, see her discuss the subject she loved so much with like-minded people. And for an instant he thought he saw a quickly concealed flash of disappointment in her eyes. Reminded himself that his plan would hopefully chase disappointment from her face and replace it with the smile that lit her whole face, released the dimple that captivated him.

'Of course,' she said easily. 'It's worked out really well that they have a guest chalet here so you can work.' She glanced out of the window and unclicked her seat belt. 'Oh look. This must be Erika and Peter now.'

Minutes later introductions were made. 'It is lovely to meet you. We are so looking forward to talking to you and showing you round. We are sorry you can't make it, Gio. I will ask Carl, our son, to show you the chalet. There is Wi-Fi and everything you should need to work.'

'Thank you.' He approached Amara, leaned down and brushed her lips with his, felt the tremor run through her body and his own. 'See you later.'

# CHAPTER TEN

AMARA GAVE A final smile to Erika who had driven her to the guest chalet in a small buggy used to drive across the vineyard. 'Thank you so much. I've had a wonderful time and I've learnt a lot. And this is beautiful,' she added, gesturing to the chalet nestled within sight of the vineyard. Another fairy tale place, a vineyard muffled in snow, resting and preparing for the following year's harvest, a place of potential and hope.

'You and Gio are welcome back any time, and if you wanted to bring your grandfather we'd be honoured to meet him.'

Amara felt her smile falter a little, recalled that it wouldn't be herself and Gio. Because once they were married, they would be living separate lives, pursuing their own goals. That was what she wanted, she reminded herself, what she could cope with. Separate lives meant they wouldn't be dependent on each other for happiness, no angst and worry over if she was doing the right thing. No trying to dismantle her protective wall, or flip a switch that was already flipped and locked on permanently off. Instead, they could live separate lives, but the time they did spend together could be care-free and easy and fun. No responsibilities or obligations.

Even so as she waved goodbye to Erika, she felt a sudden fillip of anxiety. Had today been about Gio needing space form her? Was she grating on his nerves? Or had she encroached too far? Was she getting this wrong?

A memory of the morning shivered over her, the feeling of waking up nestled next to him, the warmth and the closeness that felt somehow magnified by everything she'd shared, emo-tionally and physically.

Remembered panic regenerated. What had happened to her wall? Because despite the comfort and the help he'd given, the idea that she'd shared such a personal part of herself, her memories of Luca, was terrifying. She didn't let people close, wouldn't risk more hurt and loss. That idea reinforced by the knowledge that her parents' seemingly idyllic marriage had been anything but. Love brought nothing but complications and she mustn't forget it.

What she needed now was distance, not proximity. And maybe Gio had felt the same. He'd spent a couple of hours with Amara and the Merz family but had then returned to the chalet to work. And she understood that, but now she wondered if it had simply been an excuse to give them both space. If so she respected that.

But despite all the thoughts, she was aware of a bubble of happiness as she approached the front door, a sense of anticipation, a desire to see him.

She quickened her pace as a flurry of snowflakes swirled down and she pushed the door open. Stood in the hallway for a second just as Gio emerged from a room on the left and closed the door behind him.

'Perfect timing,' he said as she hung her coat up on the hook, aware of a sudden sense of awkwardness. Should she step forward and kiss him or was that not appropriate? She was pretty sure throwing herself into his arms when it was just the two of them would send the wrong signal. In the end, she settled for a smile and a raised eyebrow in question. 'I'm getting dinner ready,' he explained. 'And you have time for a relaxing bath.' He stepped forward and pulled her into a quick kiss, a kiss that dizzied her, distracted her. 'The bathroom is down the hall on the left,' he said and she nodded, her heart still beating extra fast as she headed to the bathroom.

Warmth doused her as she saw Gio had laid out a fluffy towel and by the bath was a bottle of luxurious bubble bath, scented with her favourite vanilla scent. She frowned. How had he even known that?

After her bath, she headed into the bedroom, a bedroom they would share, the idea sending a thrill through her as she thought about what to wear. Wanted to make sure it was something that would distract Gio as much as his kiss had distracted her, would make it clear that she was more than up for a repeat of the night before.

In the end, she settled for one of her new purchases. A red flower–printed dress, with a lace underlay, long-sleeved and high-necked but falling to mid-thigh, it combined demure and sexy, especially when paired with open-toed, black high heels.

As she surveyed her reflection, she barely recognised herself as the woman who'd packed to escape to the Bavarian Alps mere days before.

Now she looked radiant, her eyes held a sparkle, a brightness, and her whole body seemed to move with more confidence, more awareness. A body that now knew so much more, knew the pleasures and joy that Gio's touch had evoked. Great sex, she reminded herself. Nothing more. A bonus factor.

But right now, those words of common sense didn't matter anymore. All she wanted was to be with Gio, enjoy his company, enjoy bantering, flirting, talking, sharing—and that was all right. Soon enough they would embark on their separate lives and until then there was no harm in revelling in these new-found sensations, the chemistry…

She walked down the corridor to find him standing near the front door, facing her, waiting for her, she realised, and now she did a double take. He looked gorgeous; his dark hair shower damp with a hint of errant curl. He'd changed into dark denim slim-cut jeans, with a black V-neck shirt under a deep grey charcoal blazer.

And now Amara didn't care about rules or appearances. All that mattered was that she was allowed to look, allowed to touch, allowed to get close. The thought seemed to occur to them both at the same time and she stepped forward just as he did, almost wonderingly. Then they were so close, so very close. 'You look stunning,' he said softly.

'And you look gorgeous,' she responded, taking one more step, let his sheer warmth, his heat, the tantalising woodsy scent of him dizzy her senses.

Then he said, 'Close your eyes. No peeking.'

She complied, and he moved behind her and she caught her breath as he gently placed his hands round her waist to guide her forward. The sound of a door opening and then she stepped forward and stopped, inhaled, aware of a glorious floral scent, the sweet scent of violets underlaid with perhaps a hint of vanilla.

'You can open them now,' he said, and she'd swear that there was a hint of nerves in his voice.

She opened her eyes and felt her mouth drop open in a small 'O' of surprise. The room had been transformed. Flowers were strategically placed around the room, the vivid purple of violets, bright red amaryllises interspersed with blooms she didn't even recognise, a riot of colour. Pillared candles of various heights were strategically placed around, adding a golden aura of illumination. The furniture had been pushed back against the walls to allow a small wooden table, liberally scattered with petals, to be the centrepiece, led to by an arched trellis. Music played in the background; music she recognised as her favourite classical composer.

Gio took her hand in his and led her to the table where a bottle of deep red wine stood and her eyes widened in further surprise as she saw the label. It was from the Rossi estate; a bottle from one of their very best yields from years before. Her absolute favourite. Already open, and Gio stepped forward and poured them both a glass and smiled at her, a smile that lit his whole face and sent a shiver through her whole body.

'This is beautiful.' For some reason she felt tears blink her eyes as she realised the thought that must have gone into this. 'How…?'

'Well, I did have to make some calls, but they weren't work-related. I called a florist, I visited a few shops, got a few things delivered and…here we are.'

'But those are my favourite flowers,' she said. 'And it must have taken ages to decorate the room like this and…' Amara made herself stop, reminded herself of their arrangement as she pulled her phone out of her pocket. 'I know this is for show, but it is really lovely of you to have gone to so much trouble to make it so…real.'

He took a step forward now. 'This *is* real.'

The words made her heart give a funny little jump and she willed her expression not to change. 'This isn't for the cameras. This is for you. To show you my thanks for agreeing to this venture, to mark another step on our way. To show you that I value you, and I admire your strength.'

He took a deep breath.

'It's also for another reason.' He took a deep breath. 'So here goes.'

Amara watched him, aware of a sudden tingle of nerves, as he moved towards the table, saw that his hand was shaking slightly as he reached out and picked up a cardboard box from the petal-strewn surface.

He stepped back towards her and she saw that the box bore the Romano Confectionery label. He opened the lid and she looked inside.

There were three Romano truffles and in the space where the fourth one should be a ring nestled.

Amara reached in with trembling fingers and took it out. 'It's beautiful,' she breathed. And it was. Double banded, one band was rose gold the other was embedded with diamonds and the sparkle of a square ruby gemstone. Amara blinked back tears at the sheer thoughtfulness. The wine, the chocolates symbolising their marriage, the choice of gemstone, her favourite colour and the colour of the wine she loved so much.

'Will you, Amara Rossi, do me the honour of becoming my lawfully wedded wife?' he asked and his voice was husky and she knew he was genuinely asking, that in a way this was her chance to back out, that he meant this as a proposal not a fait accompli.

A mixture of emotion swirled through her. A happiness she knew to be out of proportion, a sudden dangerous sadness that this *was* all about the law. Gio needed a lawfully wedded wife. *Enough.* Amara refused to even acknowledge the sadness, refused to allow such a pointless, irrational emotion any headspace. This marriage was what she wanted, what she had agreed to willingly.

This partnership.

And dammit they were going to be happy. And so, in this moment she would only allow happiness in, would believe in their happy ever after.

'Yes. I will marry you.'

'Thank you.' His smile crinkled and lit his brown eyes. 'I know this isn't a conventional proposal and I won't insult you by saying words that neither of us wants or means or needs, but please believe all of this is not for show or the cameras. I have no intention of taking a single photo—this is truly for you. For us. This is the only proposal I propose to make in my life and I hope it is the only one you will ever receive because I truly want to make this work.'

'So do I.' She lifted her glass of wine. 'The perfect choice.'

'For the perfect bride.' He reached out and picked up the ring and she held her hand out, and as he slipped the ring onto her finger, she felt something she couldn't quite identify jolt through her and quickly she turned away from him slightly, under the pretext of holding her hand up so the gemstones caught the light.

'Does it fit?' he asked. 'I had to guess your ring size.'

'It's slightly loose but only slightly. And I love it, the design… Everything. I love all of this. But how on earth could you know that this is my favourite wine, that this is my favourite music…?'

He smiled at her. 'I have a source,' he said. 'I spoke with your grandfather.'

Amara stared at him.

'I asked his permission to ask for your hand in marriage. Old-fashioned, I know, but I thought… Well, I thought it would make it easier for you if I paved the way. I know how worried you are about lying to him.'

Now Amara didn't even bother to try to blink back the tears. 'You did that?'

'Yes. It was very nerve-wracking, but I'm glad I spoke with him. He is a real gentleman. We had a good chat. I like him very much and I think, I hope, he approved of me. He did say that he would never stand in the way of your decisions, or interfere, but he did also give us his blessing and he is looking forward to us going there in a few days.'

Relief washed over Amara, along with a sudden fuzzy feeling that everything really was going to be all right.

'Thank you,' she said softly. 'I truly mean that. It makes all of this even more special and precious than it already was.' And she didn't care if her words could be misinterpreted. This was precious. It did mark the start of their marriage. And it was a good, auspicious start.

'You're very welcome.' Now he grinned; the type of grin that sent a warmth of a different sort over her skin. 'And if you're looking of ways to show your appreciation, I can think of a few.'

She grinned at him. 'Well please feel free to share. Or better yet, why don't you show me.'

Reaching out she took his hand, 'Let's go to bed. I wouldn't want you to lose the thread of your thoughts. And for the record, I am feeling very grateful indeed.'

An hour later and Gio watched as Amara stretched luxuriously, gloriously unselfconscious and oh, so very beautiful. A beauty that seemed to pierce his heart as he studied her, so relaxed, a smile on her face that he knew was mirrored on his. A smile of satiation, contentment and sheer awe at the sensations experienced over the past minutes, passion, joy, yearning, sheer voluptuous pleasure. He saw the glint of the ring on her finger, his ring, a symbol of commitment and felt a fierce pride that this woman had agreed to marry him. No matter what the motivation, no matter that it was a ring of convenience, it bound them together. She was his.

She smiled lazily at him and he grinned back. 'How about we stay right here and eat dinner in bed?'

'That works for me,' she said

'I'll be right back.' His grin widened as she gave an admiring whistle as he climbed out of bed and another when he returned ten minutes later carefully balancing a tray.

'Perfect. I'm guessing my grandfather told you my favourite food too.'

'Well, he gave me a choice and I went for the one I thought I could manage to cook most easily,' he admitted.

'This looks incredible. I love Spaghettini Verdi.' She twirled up a forkful and sighed happily. 'Exactly the right proportions of parsley and Parmesan,' she said. 'And this is proper Parmesan, as well.'

Once they had eaten, they sat propped up against the headboard, their legs pressed together, her hair tickling his shoulder and she sipped her wine, then made an exclamation of annoyance. 'The ring. It must have fallen off whilst I was eating.' Quickly she rummaged around in the bed and found it, put it on the bedside table, suddenly scared that she would lose it. 'So, what now?' she asked. 'Now we are officially engaged.'

'We'll announce our engagement. I'll get that sorted in the morning and we can put it on social media. Then we're meeting your grandfather in a few days and I'd like you to meet my grandparents, as well.'

He felt her stiffen a little bit beside him and he took her hand.

'Don't worry. They aren't scary.'

'I know. I'm just worried I'll mess this up. I know how important this is to you. How much you care about them. I don't want to say the wrong thing or let them see how angry I am that they excluded you from your birthright. And I'm worried in case your father or brothers are there. I know how important it is to make this believable to them. What if I let you down?'

The very fact that she had asked the question twisted his chest, brought home the knowledge of what he was asking her to do. Yes, he had to put on a show, but his show was for the benefit of Vittorio Rossi, a gentleman who had behaved with honour, a man who truly loved his granddaughter and would welcome Gio Rossi into the family. *Gio* was expecting Amara to put on a show for his grandparents, who were essentially happy for her to be used as a pawn on the Romano chessboard. He was going to expose her to the manipulation and scrutiny of his father, a man he knew to be an unscrupulous bully. Even though Gio *knew* he would protect her, would never let his father even whisper the hint of an insult… *knew* his grandparents would treat Amara with respect and civility at a minimum, *knew* she would be living her own life, the idea still jarred.

He took a deep breath. 'Perhaps it would be better if you didn't get too involved with my family. Maybe you don't have to actually meet my grandparents and…'

'Okay.' Her voice was small and he felt her body flinch, saw her face take on a sudden shuttered look. 'Maybe you're right. It's better that way. To keep a distance. Make sure we don't get too involved in each other's lives.'

Gio blinked, considered her words. Was she right? The idea of this marriage was that they lived independently, didn't have any of the complications that went with emotional entanglement. Yes, they needed the marriage to look real, but his grandparents were aware that it wasn't. So did she need to meet them right now? At some point she would need to meet his father, but not instantly. Another thought hit him. Was this her way of saying that she didn't *want* him to come with her to meet Lorenzo? Accepted the *necessity* that it was *needed* to keep Vittorio happy, but it wasn't what she wanted. That she didn't want him to be part of her world? That idea also jarred, it hurt because he wanted to be there, by her side.

But was that too much—was that infringing on the rules, the underlying principle of their agreement? A principle that perhaps she wanted him to honour; a principle that meant of course Amara didn't want him to be an intrinsic part of *her* life.

Gio glanced at her, saw the shadows, the questions in her eyes and alongside that he also saw hurt. Maybe *she* was hurt, maybe she thought he didn't *want* her to meet his grandparents.

Too many questions.

'Amara…' he began.

Just as she said, 'It's okay, Gio. You don't have to explain. I understand if you don't want to take the risk of me meeting them. I may mess it up…'

Huh? Now all thoughts of independent lives flew out of the window, even as a fleeting alarm bell told him to stop, to think, to at least file the thoughts away for later. But all that mattered now was clearing up the misunderstanding.

'That's not what I meant,' he said. 'I don't think you'll mess up.'

'Then why?'

'Because if things get difficult, get nasty, it's not fair on you.'

'So, you're protecting me?'

'I'm being fair. Why should I expect you to embroil yourself in my family dramas?'

'Because you'd be a fool not to embroil me. Me meeting your grandparents, your family, bolsters our whole pretence—that this marriage is real. You do need your father to believe it or he will have ammunition to try to keep you off the board. So right now, I don't need protecting. I don't want protecting. I want to keep my side of our marriage deal.'

Amara was right, but it still felt wrong. Not when she didn't know what she was letting herself in for.

'Okay,' he nodded. 'But if you are going to do this then you need to know the truth. About my family.'

She laid a hand on his arm. 'You don't have to tell me, Gio.'

'Yes, I do.' That at least did feel right.

Amara turned to face him, her face serious now, still flushed, but her eyes were soft, focused on him and he knew she would really hear him. He took a moment to think about what he wanted to say, oh, so aware that he had never shared this with anyone; that he was revisiting memories that he had held at bay for years.

'Okay. Here goes.'

# CHAPTER ELEVEN

AMARA WAITED, knew that what Gio was about to share was intensely personal, could see shadows crowd his brown eyes, the rigidity of his jaw, the tension in his body, oh, so close to her own.

'I told you that I felt I owed my grandparents. For being there for me, for acknowledging me. But I owe them for more than that. My grandparents stepped in when no one else did, when I thought no one else would.'

She didn't push him, waited for him to be ready to explain further.

'I told you about my parents' wedding. It was a marriage my father deeply regretted mostly because it brought about my existence. Otherwise he could have written it off as youthful folly. As it was it lumbered him with me. Literally. Thanks to my mother insisting on joint custody, my father and his family were stuck with a physical reminder of my existence on an ongoing basis.'

'They were also your family,' she said quietly. 'Your father's sons were your half-siblings.' Just like Lorenzo and Daisy were hers. The knowledge a sudden pinprick of guilt, but also of a shift in feeling.

'They didn't see it that way.' She could hear the underlying bitterness in his voice, saw him try to smile, to soften his tone. 'It was difficult for my father and stepmother and it was difficult for me, because…they made it obvious how they felt about me.'

'Obvious how?' Her voice was neutral, neither judgemental nor pitying.

'They allowed my brothers to bully me, at first it was letting them get away with what they called "rough and tumble", but it wasn't play fighting. It was more one of them pinning me down and the other one putting the boot in. And my dad and my stepmother, Bianca, would look the other way. Then it slowly escalated. Ignoring it evolved into active encouragement. Every visit things got a little bit worse, almost as if my stepbrothers were pushing the boundaries of what they could do. I will say though that my father and stepmother were never physically abusive themselves. It was more what they said, how they treated me. Mind games, ways of making me feel different. Inferior. Taunts. My brothers would play a game of consequences where basically they could choose what forfeit I had to pay if I did anything "wrong". If I smiled it was a smirk—if I didn't smile, I was sulking. It all cost a forfeit. My father and stepmother would think it was all hilarious. They'd do everything they could to make it clear that I was different.'

Amara listened in growing disbelief that anyone could behave to a child that way, to any child let alone your own flesh and blood. How could Salvatore Romano have let it happen? And what must it have done to Gio, the constant humiliations, the sense of inferiority, of being second-class? She could almost see the small dark-haired boy stoic and hurt, refusing to cry, perhaps even thinking it was true, that he deserved the treatment meted out to him.

'It all sounds daft really,' he added.

'No, it doesn't.' Amara tried to control her voice, but she couldn't, could hear the choke of anger, the outrage. 'It sounds vindictive and mean and bullying and downright wrong.' Her hands clenched into fists. 'You did not deserve to be treated like that, Gio.'

'I know.' But he didn't; she could see it in his eyes, the doubt, the questions. His head might tell him she was right but somewhere deep inside him that small boy still lived on.

'Good. Because you deserved love and if they couldn't give you that then there is something wrong with them. You are his son. But if for some reason he couldn't love you he could at least have shown you respect and kindness and civility.' The words had an echo to them, resonated, and she blinked, realised that that was what they were basing their marriage on. The idea sent a sudden discomfort through her and she pushed it away. This was about Gio, not about them.

'I think that's what my grandfather thought, too,' he said. 'He arrived at the house unexpectedly one day and came in. He saw what was happening and he…well, he made it all stop. I don't know how. He asked me to leave the room and wait by the front door. Half an hour later he came to the door and took me back to his house.'

'Did your father talk to you about it?'

'Nope. Nobody did, not even my grandfather. I have no idea what my father said to my grandfather. I assume he played it down. I assumed he blamed it on me somehow. But whatever they said, from then on things changed. My grandparents would invite me to stay with them sometimes.'

Amara could hear the surprise in his voice and it tugged at her heart that all these years later the idea that someone could actually want his company could cause Gio surprise. No wonder he saw relationships as deals, things to be controlled and negotiated.

'And the visits to my father were different.' He shrugged. 'We were all marking time until I was old enough for the visits to stop. They pretty much ignored me. I mean there were still sighs, and dirty looks, but on the whole, they left me alone.'

Amara took his hand. 'I'm guessing in some ways that hurt too.'

He nodded and she thought he'd withdraw his hand and she increased the pressure of her hold, wanted him to know that she was there, wasn't going anywhere.

'I guess at first, I hoped that somehow my grandfather had worked a miracle, somehow made everything change, make them if not love me at least like me. But that's not possible—you can't make people like you and you certainly can't make them love you.'

'No. You can't. But it sounds as though your grandparents loved you.'

There was a silence and she could see the confusion in his eyes. 'I think they… Care about me. I think they always felt they had some sort of moral duty towards me. And I admire them for calling my father out when no one else did. I tried to tell my mother, but she didn't want to believe me, didn't want to rock the boat. Because it might have meant she would have been required to have me with her more.'

Amara placed her hand on his, wondered how Luna Rocca could have justified being so caught up in her own life that she had ignored the pleas of her own son.

'My grandparents did do something, but I know that was hard for them. My father is their only son, their pride and joy, their blood. To believe ill of him wouldn't have come easy. It would have been easy to ignore. They didn't. But…' He hesitated.

'But you believe they somehow blame you?' Her voice was gentle now, her heart twisting further as she followed the logic the young Gio had followed.

'Yes. After all, my father cared for his second wife, cared for my brothers. He certainly never mistreated them. They were a unit, a family. I brought out the worst in him. I created the problem. Or at least, I was the catalyst.'

'No.' Amara's voice was firm. 'Your father

and stepmother created the problem. They had no right to treat you like that. None at all.' But she could see how easy it was for Gio to blame himself. A distant mother and a father who despised him; he'd concluded he was the problem. 'It wasn't you,' she said again. 'You did nothing wrong. You didn't turn your father into a bully—his actions are on him. You say they were a family unit and maybe they were, but what he and your stepmother did was wrong on so many fronts. They brought your half-brothers up to be bullies, encouraged them to inflict pain and hurt—that in itself is a travesty of parenting, shows no understanding of what family means.'

He glanced at her and she could see that this hadn't occurred to him. That for him, his father's house had simply been a place of torment, a place where he was the one outside the 'true' family unit. The one who deserved to be treated badly.

'It is not on you,' she repeated. Hoped she'd got through.

'Either way I won't let my grandparents suffer from his bullying tactics.'

'I agree with that.' Whatever their faults, and she couldn't absolve them fully, they had been the best people in Gio's childhood. 'And I want to help. I will not let you down and I will be by your side.'

The words echoed around the room and for a few moments they sat, hands clasped and as she looked down at their joined hands a sudden sense of strength, of togetherness, of connection seemed to shimmer and solidify.

Then he squeezed her hand and said, 'Come on.'

'Where to?'

'A starlit walk. You can show me the vineyard and we can think about the future. Our future. Because we're going to make this work, and I want our engagement night to be full of a whole plethora of memories, of great sex, confidences, sharing the past and looking forward to the future.'

'I love that idea.' And she did. Suddenly wondered if she would have loved any plan that involved being with Gio. Decided it didn't matter. She didn't care. She wanted to walk by starlight hand in hand and think about the future, their future. Yes, she knew medium-term they would have individual separate paths, but for now she could see that for a while there was a good reason for them to be together. For a while they *needed* to be together. *Needed* to make sure the wool was pulled over Salvatore

Romano's eyes. The idea filled her with a disproportionate happiness and a danger signal clanged.

But there was no danger. There was no choice; they needed to do this. The fact that she wanted to do it was a bonus, surely. Once Gio was established, once Salvatore accepted their marriage as real, they would both back off. By then they would both want to. Sorted. So in the meantime, why not focus on the moment, the job in hand. She of all people knew there was little point dwelling on the future.

Half an hour later they were outside and she gathered her thoughts, tried to sound brisk and professional.

'I think the best plan is to make sure that we look the part for at least a few months. That way your father shouldn't suspect anything whilst you establish yourself. From a practical viewpoint I am happy to spend time with you, getting to know your grandparents better.'

'I'd appreciate that, but I also want to be at the vineyard. I know you are needed there.'

She shrugged and for the first time she said the words without minding. 'Yes, but my grandfather will be there and I suppose that Lorenzo and Daisy will be spending time there too. So I will need to be at the vineyard for some of the time, but…'

'*We* will need to be there,' he corrected gently. 'I have no intention of leaving you to face Lorenzo and Daisy on your own. Not until we have figured them out.'

Amara looked up at the glitter and gleam of the stars. And despite the knowledge that it was all part of the deal, happiness welled up inside her and she wondered if indeed the stars had aligned to bring her and Gio together.

'That sounds like a plan,' she said and as he bent to kiss her, she knew she would always remember this starlit night and the feel of his lips on hers.

Amara woke up, opened her eyes, intensely aware that the space beside her was empty. Panic touched her and she told herself not to be foolish. Gio had probably gone to the bathroom or to start breakfast or maybe he wanted some space.

Memories of the previous night washed over her, the way they had held each other, had fallen asleep in each other's arms, and she knew her dreams had been happy. Images of walks around the vineyard with Gio, cooking dinner with Gio, meal planning, choosing restaurants, standing side by side. Gio and Amara. Amara and Gio. And now, still half asleep, other images streamed her mind, herself holding a baby. A tiny, perfect scrap of humanity with Gio's dark hair, cradled in her arms and Gio standing next to her, looking down at the infant with love and pride.

Now she sat up; that was taking things way too far. Yet why? Why couldn't all those dreams become reality? The question, the fact she'd even thought it, poleaxed her and she stilled, one hand clenched around the sheet. But somehow the sense of happiness, contentment, the sense of possibilities and potential remained. Other people experienced real happy ever afters, maybe she actually could? Because she'd never felt like this before, never been so comfortable with anyone, never felt so close, so connected. Why should it go wrong? If fate had brought them together, perhaps fate could keep them together.

The idea was too big, too enormous, too much to contemplate and she swung her legs out of bed. Headed for the bathroom where she showered quickly, dressed and headed to the kitchen. Despite herself anticipation showed in the goofy smile she felt upturn her lips, as somehow the idea of being a couple, of being

Amara and Gio, Gio and Amara still permeated her brain. But as she approached there was no noise, no waft of coffee or toast coming from the kitchen and she told herself she shouldn't expect breakfast to be prepared for her. Yet a small worry surfaced as she listened, was suddenly very sure she was alone in the house.

A belated glance at her watch showed her that it was ridiculously late; she couldn't recall the last time she had slept so deeply and now a vague memory surfaced, a sense of Gio stood over her, a fleeting gentle kiss that had sent a flutter of happiness through her without fully waking her. A dream or reality?

She pushed the kitchen door open, saw that it was indeed empty, though a rinsed-out mug showed that Gio had had coffee before leaving. He'd also taken the trouble to clean the kitchen from the night before.

And now she spotted a note on the kitchen table, moved over to read it.

> Amara, I have headed into Munich to have your ring altered for you. I was going to wake you up to see if you wanted to come, but you looked so asleep I thought I would leave you. I will bring back some extra

breakfast (breakfast in bed?) I shouldn't be back late, I am aiming to be there when the shops open. Gio

So, he must have set off pretty early and he should be back any minute now. But as the minutes began to stretch she became aware of a sense of worry, an edginess that she tried to alleviate with a cup of tea, another cup of tea, recleaning the already clean kitchen, and eventually she messaged him. Tried not to sound clingy or needy.

Looked up as she heard the ting of a message being received and then she spotted it. Gio had left his phone behind, he must have been charging it and forgotten to pick it up. The idea should have made her feel better. He'd just been held up and couldn't let her know. Yet somehow panic was beginning to churn inside her, and she checked the local news, stared down at what she saw and now panic crystallised and surged into a tsunami.

There'd been a pile-up; she saw the images of firefighters, ambulances, police, tried to make head or tail of it all, desperately Google translating, checking maps and all the while panic getting worse and worse.

There had been a crash, there were fatalities,

it was the road that Gio would have been on at some point in his journey. She made frantic calculations as she paced up and down, forced herself to try and work out timelines, tried to tell herself he was caught in traffic, couldn't contact her. That he was all right. He had to be all right.

But she knew how fate could work, how a series of random events, a ring that was a size too big, a ring that had slipped off her finger, a man who had woken up early, perhaps motivated by a sense of edginess after a night of spilling his soul. A man who happened to be located on a Bavarian vineyard because he happened to be engaged to a wine heiress. Domino after domino. Because the dominoes of fate had fallen for some people; there were people who had died.

She tried to think, she had to work out how to get to him. Up and down, trying to block out images that filled her with pain and horror. Perhaps she could call the hospital, call a helpline call…call who? There was nothing she could do, but wait and pace and pray and try to block out memories, memories of loss and pain and grief. Of finding her grandfather, his face streaked with tears. Her grandfather, a man who never showed emotion, didn't cry.

He'd held his grief to himself but she'd seen it. Seen what losing a loved one did. Even now she hadn't healed from all the loss. Losing Luca. Now what if she'd lost Gio?

He might be lying somewhere dead, caught in a wreckage, his body twisted and splayed. He may be gone. The thought tore at her insides, hollowed her out with pain. How could fate have done this? Further pain ratcheted as she realised her own involvement, how fate had used her. Because she was part of the domino effect. If she hadn't agreed to marry him then Gio wouldn't have bought the ring in the first place. Hell, if she'd only thought to give him her ring size. If, if, if… That's how fate worked, worked to use events and people and cause accidents that wrenched happiness from people. That's why she understood it was better to walk alone, to remain safe behind a wall. Because she knew now it didn't just protect her. It protected others, kept her from becoming a domino in fate's hands. She should never have agreed to this arrangement. Never have done this, and then Gio would be alive and well. This had all been a mistake, she'd let Gio close, allowed herself to dream.

Now how bitterly she regretted those dreams, those illusions of happiness. How bitterly she regretted letting him so close, allowing a connection, allowing herself to care. And as she paced, Amara knew she couldn't do this; made a deal with herself. If Gio lived, if Gio was all right, Amara would release him from this. Would release herself from what commitment brought. Release them both. Would walk away before she actually married him, brought them even closer, spent more time together.

Her vision of earlier came back to mock her. Herself and Gio as parents. She couldn't be a mother, because she wouldn't be able to protect her baby from the unpredictability of fate. Would coddle them, wouldn't know how to parent without wrapping them in cotton wool, making their lives miserable with her anxieties. As for herself and Gio, Amara and Gio, Gio and Amara, the words took on a taunting rhythm.

Up and down she paced, the horrific images unfiltered now. Nothing was worth this risk, the risk of this type of loss. But first, please God let him be all right.

And then finally, finally she saw the front door swing open and she leapt to her feet.

Gio pushed the front door open, knew that Amara must be wondering where he'd gone.

It had been daft to leave his phone behind but when he'd left, he hadn't really been thinking practically. The previous night had blown him away, made sleep difficult. He'd felt so much lighter sharing his past, and it was as though the connection between them was fizzing and sparking, becoming more solid, more visible, more real. And that had made him feel…energised.

A bit fizzy himself, full of energy, a need to keep going forward, without thinking too hard. But when he'd seen how asleep Amara looked a protective sense had prevailed, a desire to keep her cocooned and safe and so he had decided to get up, and then he'd figured he might as well do something proactive. And also, he wanted his ring to be on her finger. It might be a convenient ring, but it proclaimed to the world that she was his fiancée and it felt… right that it should sit on her finger securely.

And so, he'd set off.

The trip to Munich had been fine; it had been the trip back that had taken a long time.

'I'm sorry…' he started and then stood back as she moved towards him, stood and stared at him as though she couldn't believe her eyes. She reached out and placed a tentative hand on his chest, then his cheek and then she heaved a great sigh and he saw the shudder run through her.

'I heard the news, that there had been an accident. I thought…'

Oh hell. She'd thought it might have been him.

'Oh, Amara, I am sorry. My phone… I should have stopped somewhere. I didn't realise why they'd closed the road. But I should have called.' He should have found a payphone, paid someone to use their mobile… Anything. Instead, he'd just wanted to get back.

'It's okay. The important thing is that you are all right. That you aren't one of those poor souls who died.' Her voice broke and he stepped forward to take her into his arms, shared her sadness at the tragedy that had plucked people's lives away with no notice, all because they were in the wrong place at the wrong time. Knew his sadness was nothing compared to Amara's. Knew all the memories it must have brought back to her. No wonder she looked so dazed.

But as he approached her, she stepped back, held one hand out and he saw something almost akin to revulsion on her face, her green eyes glittered now with something he couldn't identify. Sadness, anger and a steely determination and yes, a rejection, a clear *do not come near me*.

Gio felt a sudden wrench of panic twist his chest, told himself to keep calm. It was completely understandable for Amara to be having all sort of reactions and emotions.

'We need to talk,' she said and now her voice was weighted, with anger and sadness.

'Okay.'

They headed into the kitchen, sat at the small table and looked out at the vineyards in the distance and he recalled their starlit conversation of the night before.

For some reason every detail of the room seemed to be etching itself on his memory as if by focusing on the detail he could put off whatever Amara was going to say. The gleam of the fridge, the jut of the marble counter, the smooth wood of the floor.

'I can't go through with this marriage.' Her voice was jerky.

'Why not?' His voice harder than he had meant it to be, but as she said each word it felt as though each one was a bullet that shattered each precious image of the future he'd been building up. Building up without even realising it.

'This morning… When I thought I'd lost you

I realised exactly why I can't deal with commitment of any sort. It's too big a risk. I can't do it. I won't do it.'

The words cut into him with unexpected ferocity. Of course she couldn't commit to him. He wasn't worth committing to, worth taking a risk on. That's what his parents had both believed. Why should Amara be any different? He should have known this couldn't work. But he hadn't expected this hurt, this pain, this bleak sadness. But his own pain didn't matter now. All he could see was Amara, her ravaged face, and from somewhere he tried to draw some reserve of strength. Because she was hurting.

'I am so sorry, Gio. I should never have agreed to this and now… Now I have wrecked things for you.' Her green eyes held panic, and he could see the clench and unclench of her hands and it killed him not to step forward and hold her, reassure her. But he couldn't, because she didn't want him to. His touch would only make things worse for her and that was another gut punch of pain. 'Maybe, maybe we can get married,' she said and his heart leapt with joy, at the hope of reprieve.

The idea he could fight back, show Amara that they could make this work. That he was worth the risk. That really nothing had changed since last night, when they'd made their plans. Wanted to face the next months side by side.

'Just on paper,' she said. 'We could go through a ceremony, then legally you'd be okay. We could come up with a story, that I'm ill or was called away for work…' Anything so that she didn't have to be near him; shades of his parents. Shades of his life. Amara didn't want to be by his side, wanted out of their arrangement. She didn't want to take the risk of commitment to him. And that was her right. He saw sadness on her face, but he also saw determination. She had made that decision, a decision to walk completely alone, to live her own life, to answer to no one but herself.

It seemed so clear to him now; somewhere down the line the rules and boundaries of their deal had blurred. Amara was right, they couldn't walk side by side and remain uninvolved, uninvested in the other. He was involved, was invested, wanted nothing more right now than her happiness. And that meant letting go. However much he didn't want to, however much he wanted to try to persuade her that it would be all right. That the risk was worth it. Because it wasn't. He wasn't. Amara had gone through so much. He wouldn't add to it, wouldn't try to force her to do something she didn't want to do.

'No,' he said. 'You don't need to do that and you haven't wrecked anything.' It all seemed so clear to him now. 'I should never have embroiled you in this. I should never have embroiled anyone. I should have worked out a different way in the first place. This whole idea was misguided from the start.' Completely misguided. He should never have asked her to do this. After all what had he done? He'd made her and himself into pawns on the Romano chessboard once again. Perhaps his motivations had been good, but his actions had been wrong. A continuation of the past. He would fight his father and he would support his grandparents, but he would find a different way. A better way.

It was time for them both to get off the chessboard. Time for him to do the right thing and let her go.

'Truly, Amara. It is all right. It's time to do this properly. Above board. So we can dissolve our arrangement. We didn't announce the engagement—the publicity will die down soon enough. This will be written off as another of my affairs.' The words so hollow he could almost feel them scoop out his insides. Logically surely, they should be true; he had only known Amara a few days, but logic seemed to have flown out of the window. Logically he shouldn't be feeling this soul-shrivelling pain, a pain that was bleak and desolate and personal.

'I will sort this out Amara. I will find a way, do what I should have done in the first place. But now what would you like to do? You are welcome to stay here, or I can drive you to the airport or…'

She shook her head. 'I'll get a taxi from here once I've sorted out a flight. I'm going home. I'll tell my grandfather the truth.' She took a deep breath, her green eyes large and stricken. 'Goodbye, Gio. I hope with all my heart that this works out for you. You are a good man and I know you will find a way.'

'Goodbye, Amara. I wish you all the luck in the world and I know you have the inner strength and courage to navigate everything, to do the best for yourself and the Rossi estate.' He managed a smile. 'I'll buy a bottle of next year's harvest.'

She stepped towards him and lifted a hand to his cheek, the touch, so brief, so fleeting but he knew it would be imprinted on him forever.

# CHAPTER TWELVE

*Two days later*
*Castle Alavario, Tuscany*

AMARA SAT OPPOSITE Vittorio Rossi in the study that she knew so well, looked round at the dark green curtains tied back with tassels of gold, at the leather-topped desk, the teak sideboard, the worn leather sofa and the patterned rug, the portraits of Rossis gone by on the walls.

Yet the items, all so familiar, gave her no comfort, seemed somehow faded and grey, like everything felt. Exactly as everything had felt since she turned her back on Gio and walked away. How could she miss anyone this much, so much that it was a dull physical ache, a constant reminder of what she'd lost? She tried not to think about him, tried to take solace from the castle, the estate. Her grandfather had taken one look at her face and simply told her to rest, take her time, talk to him when and if she was ready. Hadn't asked her where Gio was, hadn't asked her anything.

And so, she'd spent two days trying and trying to erase the memories, trying to tell herself she'd made the right decision. After all, if it hurt this much now, how much more would it have hurt later down the line?

She didn't even understand why it hurt so much. Her relationships with Stefan and Silvio had lasted over a year and she'd tried to get close, wanted to let them in. But when those relationships had ended, she'd been disappointed in herself, made sad by her own shortcomings. She hadn't missed them at all. They had barely scratched the surface. Whereas Gio, in a scant few days, had got under her skin. No, he'd done way more than that—he'd got into her heart, her soul…he'd somehow connected to her. A connection she could feel, would swear still shimmered and simmered between her and him, wherever he was at this moment. She closed her eyes, told herself that it would fade, and eventually surely it would dissipate, dissolve, disappear. It would just take time… And then somehow, one day she'd be alone and happy in her solitude.

'Amara?' Vittorio's voice was gentle. 'You said you wanted to talk.'

Amara nodded, knew she owed her grandfather an explanation.

'I assume the marriage isn't happening?' he asked, his voice devoid of judgement or censure and yet guilt swirled an extra layer into the fog of misery that engulfed her. She'd raised her grandfather's hopes, deceived him and now she couldn't follow through. She'd let him down, let Gio down.

She shook her head. 'I'm sorry, Nonno. I know you must be disappointed in me. I should have gone through with it. Or I should never have agreed to marry Gio.' But looking back, even knowing what she knew now, even when every heartbeat seemed to hurt, when everything, every scent, every taste reminded her of him, even now she couldn't regret the past few days.

Remembered how he'd held her, his smile, the deep brown of his eyes, how he looked when he was asleep, his laugh, his touch. Every second of her time with him etched into a treasure trove of bittersweet memories.

'Why did you agree?'

'It was a business arrangement. He needed a wife for business reasons. I wanted to make you happy, provide you with reassurance that I wouldn't be alone when you died. I wanted support so that I wouldn't be outnumbered by Lorenzo and Daisy.' She gave a small helpless shrug. 'It seemed like a good idea at the time. I'm sorry. Sorry I lied to you, sorry I raised your hopes.'

'Amara you have no need to apologise to me. Not now, not ever. I do love the estate and of course I hope that there will always be a Rossi at the helm. But I know too that the world does not hinge on it. I would give up the whole Rossi estate in a heartbeat if it could bring our family back. I would give it up just to spend one more day with your grandmother, to have had a chance to tell her how much she meant to me. But that tragedy, the only good thing from it was, *is* you Amara. You were spared and I thank God every day for that. You have brought my life joy. I wouldn't change anything about you. It is enough for me that you are here. If you wish to do something different with your life that is okay with me—if you marry, if you have children that is up to you. I simply want your happiness.' Amara blinked back tears, reached out and touched her grandfather's arm.

'Thank you, Nonno. You have always been my rock, my anchor. I couldn't have survived without you.'

'As for Lorenzo and Daisy, I do want to welcome them to our family. I do hope to build a relationship with them, but not at the cost of your happiness. Forgive me Amara, I did not realise how much their arrival would affect you.' He hesitated. 'Is that why you are so unhappy?'

'No.' Amara answered without thinking. 'They aren't the reason why.' The words the truth. Her time with Gio, hearing how his half-siblings had treated him. Hearing how his family had treated him because they resented him, feared him, regretted his existence…somehow without her even realising it it had caused her own resentment against her siblings to fade away. 'I want to give them a chance.'

'I am glad. But then, Amara, what is causing your unhappiness? If you feel guilty about me, I hope I have made you see that there is no need.'

'You have, Nonno. It's not that either.' Her unhappiness was caused by missing Gio. She had to assume that one day work, her grandfather, perhaps even her siblings would give her purpose. That one day she'd smile again, but right now the idea that she would never see Gio again was a sheer, bleak knowledge of a future that seemed desolate.

'Then what is wrong?'

The kindness, the concern, the love in his voice undid her resolve to say nothing. 'I… I miss Gio,' she blurted out. 'It's foolish, ridiculous and I know it will pass.' She gulped, blinked hard and then forced a smile to her face. 'I think it was all a bit much. Truly, I will be fine.'

'I am sure you will, but… I don't understand. Why did you decide not to marry Gio? You said you couldn't go through with it. I thought that meant you decided you couldn't enter a loveless business marriage.'

Amara shook her head. 'I couldn't marry him, because I couldn't take the risk of losing him.' Couldn't risk losing the man she loved. *Loved.* The word resonated round her brain, ricocheted and echoed as she tried to encompass the meaning.

There was a silence before Vittorio spoke and when he did his voice was gentle but none the less fervent for all that. 'But you have lost him already.'

Amara shook her head. 'I know, but time will heal the pain and I will be okay on my own again.'

'So you would sacrifice love, sacrifice happiness with another.'

'Yes. To avoid the pain you went through

when you lost Nonna, to avoid the pain I went through losing our whole family, losing Luca. How can I take the risk? And what if something goes wrong, if fate steps in and causes tragedy? What if by being with him I cause that tragedy?'

'You can't think like that. You cannot let the ifs and buts take over your life. I will not make this decision for you, Amara, of course I cannot. But I will tell you this. Despite the pain of losing your *nonna*, I would never want to undo the love we had, and I know she would feel the same way if the situation had been reversed. I would always choose love, would always take the risk. Of course there are no guarantees that you will be lucky enough to live happily ever after into old age. But love, love brings you alive. It brings joy and I would never advise you to turn your back on it.'

Just as he hadn't. Amara thought about what Gio's family had done; they *had* elected to turn their backs on loving him. His mother had chosen her own lifestyle, his father had chosen bitterness and bullying. But her grandfather, despite losing so much, his wife, his only child, his grandson, his daughter-in-law, had found it in his heart to love Amara. To take that risk. To embrace joy.

'But even if you are right…' And she wasn't sure, was still trying to come to terms with the fact she loved Gio. The fact that she was capable of love, that somehow the switch had flipped to on, enabled her to feel, to care, to connect, to love. 'It doesn't matter. Gio doesn't love me. He needed to be married. He doesn't want love.' And she couldn't marry him knowing love was one-sided. So in truth this knowledge simply made everything worse.

'Doesn't want love?' Vittorio sounded perplexed. 'How can anyone not want love?'

Amara opened her mouth to answer, then closed it again. Perhaps Gio simply didn't believe he deserved love, didn't believe love was possible for him. And who could blame him? The closest he'd got was his grandparents, two people who Amara still felt ambivalent about. They had given Gio time, perhaps some form of affection, practical help because they owed him a moral duty of care. Where was the joy, the real love in that?

And Gio did deserve love. In the time they'd had together he'd held her, listened to her, really listened, made her laugh, made her happy. Shown her things about herself she'd never have known. Given her perspective. Given her joy. She wanted him to know that. However terrifying the idea was.

'Thank you,' she said to her grandfather. 'Truly. Thank you.'

She dropped a kiss on his cheek and left the room, for the first time in days the weight, the density of misery had diffused.

*Milan. A café*

Gio wondered if this was a good idea. Wondered if they would even come to meet him. Max and Antonio Romano, his half-siblings. Would he even recognise them if they did turn up? After all he hadn't seen them in ten years. He wished, really wished, that Amara was here. He'd been so close, so very close to calling her. To tell her his plan. Tell her he'd figured it all out. Possibly. Thank her for her input.

Those words she'd said. That his brothers had been brought up to be bullies. Taught that it was the right way to be, a way to win their parents' approval. That was wrong, and it was an aspect that had never occurred to Gio. That the real Romano family unit was a 'travesty'. Perhaps because to him real Romanos could do no wrong, or because maybe he craved his father's approval himself, or maybe because it had been so painful to endure his brother jibes, taunts and fists. But in the past days he had thought and he'd realised his brothers too had been manipulated just as much as Gio had been.

He looked up as the café door opened, saw a man walk in. A man who looked familiar, both from memory and from his own reflection. Gio rose as the man approached.

'Antonio?' he hazarded the guess, thought it was the younger of his brothers.

'Gio.' His brother hesitated and held out a hand, Gio hesitated and then took it.

'Is Max coming?'

Antonio shook his head. 'Papa told us both to ignore your invitation.'

'Yet you're here?'

'Yes.'

'Why?'

'Curiosity, but also…' Now suddenly Antonio looked very young, though Gio knew he must be twenty-five. 'I want to apologise.' The words stiff, jerky, yet they held sincerity as Antonio held his gaze, though Gio could see the effort it took. 'The way we treated you was wrong.' Antonio released a breath, and his jaw lost some tension.

'Thank you.' Gio wasn't sure what else to

say, knew that everything couldn't be cancelled out with a few words; he still couldn't be sure Antonio didn't have an ulterior motive. But somehow, it felt like a start. And again, he wished so hard that Amara was here to share this event, this potential massive step forward. The hurt multiplying, deepening at the thought of never sharing anything with her again.

*Boardroom of Gio's med-tech company*

Three days after his meeting with Antonio, Gio looked across at his grandparents, could see the signs of strain, the lines of tiredness on Ava's face, the slight stoop to Aurelio's usually upright posture. He took a deep breath, knew he had to put aside his own sadness, a sadness that seemed to have seeped into his body and soul. Who knew muscles could ache from grief, feel heavy and uncoordinated. Who knew his very soul could feel so…so forlorn. Each day it seemed to get worse as if each further hour of life without Amara made the pain increase. All because she had exited his life. A woman he'd known a scant few days who had turned his world upside down, upended his beliefs and given him the courage to do this.

'Is this a good idea, Gio?' Aurelio asked.

'I think so.' In truth he didn't know. 'But if this doesn't work, I will find another way. I will not let your business go under.' And he meant it. 'But it is your business,' he said quietly. 'Yours and my father's and my brothers'. It was never mine.' Amara had been right to tell him that his love for his own company was worth something. He had built it up, he had plans for it, a passion and a drive to bring his technology to all corners of the globe, where it could do the most good. Had the ambition and the impetus to make new cutting-edge discoveries at the helm of his own company.

Aurelio opened his mouth and Gio raised a hand. 'It's okay,' he said gently.

'No, Gio. It isn't. I was wrong.' Gio stilled; they weren't words he had ever expected to hear from his grandfather. But he sensed they were important words, not only for him, but for Aurelio, and so he remained silent, let the older man continue. 'I want to say this now when it is just us, before the others get here. So you know I am not saying it as a ploy, or a move.'

'*We* were wrong, then and now,' Ava interjected. She glanced at Aurelio and then met Gio's gaze. 'We have talked a lot the past few days. Talked and reflected.' She took a deep breath. 'Salvatore was…he is our only child.

I always wanted a large family, but it wasn't meant to be. So he became our world and we… or maybe I, could see no wrong in him. But that doesn't excuse what we did to you. Somehow it was only after my diagnosis, when I know I will lose so much it seems important to look back on my past with true eyes.'

'Our past,' Aurelio said. 'And you, Gio, you didn't deserve how we treated you. To exclude you like we did.'

'And then to snap our fingers twenty-eight years later and expect you to come to our rescue.' Ava looked at him 'To expect you to get married without love or even affection.'

Gio took a deep breath, emotions roller-coasting inside him and again how he wished Amara was here. 'Thank you, for what you have just said. It means more to me than I can tell you, but as for the getting married part…' Gio gave a sudden smile. 'It wasn't like that. I promise you. Amara and I…'

Now Aurelio frowned and he saw Ava's blue eyes spark. 'Amara and you…?'

'It doesn't matter.'

'Yes. It does.' Ava reached out and took her husband's hand and they exchanged a smile, so full of love and affection that Gio felt something twist inside him. He suddenly missed

Amara with an intensity so fierce he had to brace himself against it, curl his hand around the edge of the boardroom table. 'Tell us about her,' his grandmother invited.

And suddenly the urge to talk about Amara, to paint a picture of her, to have an excuse to think about her overwhelmed him, even as he knew he should be focused on the meeting ahead.

'She is beautiful,' he said. 'I don't just mean on the outside, though she is—she is beautiful on the inside, as well. When I see her my breath catches, my heart leaps and I feel… happy.'

Ava frowned. 'I thought you told us you didn't want to marry her? That you didn't believe deception was the right way forward. That a false marriage was wrong. That there was a better way forward.'

'It is wrong and there is a better way forward for Romano Confectionery. And I don't want to marry her because marriage isn't for me. Not the real thing.'

'Why not?' Ava asked.

Gio shrugged. 'Why aren't I a real Romano? Sometimes things are just the way they are.'

'No.' Ava's voice was strong now, the lines of strain gone. 'Gio. Listen to me. My future doesn't look good. But right here, right now, I have full capacity and I want you to remember what I have to say. I want you to remember me for something good I have done for you.' She shook her head as he tried to speak. 'Firstly, you are a real Romano. No, you are actually better than that. We Romanos are hardly something to aspire to. You are a good person in your own right. You would have been justified in turning your back on us, but you haven't. You have gone on to make a massive success of your life. In your own right. You've made a difference. And I am proud of you, Gio. And the real thing is for you. You deserve to love and be loved. If you love Amara tell her. If you feel there is a chance she loves you back, then fight for her.'

Aurelio nodded. 'Your grandmother, as always, is right. Once, many years ago, I fell in love with the beautiful woman who came into my family bakery. But it took me a long while to convince her I was genuine. That I meant it. She thought I was after her recipe. Then she refused to believe I would defy my parents to marry her. It took me time to gain her trust. But I did. And I have never once regretted it. Love is a precious thing. If you've found it, give it a chance. I don't know how Amara feels about you, but if you love her give that love a chance.'

Gio stared at them. If he loved Amara. The penny clanged down. Of course he loved her, loved her with every fibre of his being. Body and soul. The idea dizzied him even as his phone buzzed followed by his PA's voice. 'Your guests are here, Gio…'

His guests, his family. Salvatore and Max and Antonio Romano.

Gio wondered if this was the worst idea he could have had, reminded himself that he had thought it all through. Knew he had to focus, had to put this bedazzling, incredible revelation aside for now. He loved Amara…and maybe she didn't want that love, but dammit he wanted to fight, wanted to tell her, wanted to share this exhilaration with her. Even if it led to rejection, he wanted her to know the truth.

The boardroom door opened just as his phone pinged in his hand. He looked down, saw the message was from Amara. His heart somersaulted, even though he had no idea what the message said. But somehow, he felt as though she were here with him as he rose to his feet to greet the Romanos. One Romano to another.

# CHAPTER THIRTEEN

AMARA COULD FEEL the butterflies ride the crest of nerves in her tummy, swooping and swirling with anxiety but also with anticipation. Because no matter what happened in the next few hours, she would be seeing Gio.

Clasping her phone, she reread their messages yet again. Tried to find any hidden meaning in them, but he'd been as careful as she to be matter of fact, prosaic.

She'd messaged and asked if they could meet. He'd agreed, asked for a time and place. She'd picked Modena, halfway between Milan and Tuscany, somewhere with no joint connotations. She'd also commandeered a small, cosy restaurant for privacy, had arrived ridiculously early to make sure everything looked right.

Perhaps it shouldn't matter, but no matter the outcome of this meeting she wanted Gio to be happy, to feel special and of value. She glanced at her watch and took one final look round. It was a restaurant she loved, owned by a friend and business colleague of her grandfather's, a man who also happened to be an award-winning chef. By a stroke of luck or perhaps fate the restaurant was closed for renovations and Enzo had been happy to allow Amara to use it.

The walls of the small, intimate dining area sported eclectic prints, a mix of local talent and famous patrons. Glorious abstracts provided splashes of colour on the white walls. The five tables all had plain white tablecloths of the most exquisite quality, four of them unadorned and unlit, the fifth the one Amara had prepared.

A bottle of red, not from the Rossi estate this time because Amara wanted this to be about Gio and herself. Two crystal glasses and a few fresh flower petals adorned the tablecloth. Simple and evocative, or at least that's what she hoped.

Her heart pounded her ribcage as the steel door swung open and there was Gio.

Amara's head whirled, and she rooted her feet to the ground, the urge to run towards him nigh on overwhelming.

'Gio,' she said. 'Thank you for agreeing to meet me here.'

'No problem.' There was an uncharacteristic hesitancy about him as he stood in the doorway. His eyes rested on her and she could see the tension in his body, could see it matched her own. 'Thank you for asking me.'

There was a silence and then Amara said, 'Come in. Sit.'

His brown eyes met hers and Amara threw caution to the wind, before they started talking about the weather or the state of the roads or their method of travel.

'I have something I need to say. Something I want to say,' she amended.

'So do I.'

He entered and approached the table and they both sat down.

'Do you want to go first?' Amara asked. Perhaps it was craven of her to offer, but maybe Gio was here to announce he'd married someone else. The idea came from nowhere and nearly toppled her off her chair, caught her breath and sent the butterflies into a frenzied swirl. 'In fact, you go first,' she said.

Gio must have heard the panic in her voice and now she saw his jaw clench, his hands flex on top of the table. And then he looked at her, really looked at her almost as if he was etching her face onto his memory, imprinting this moment on his brain and Amara was caught in his gaze. Saw such seriousness of purpose in his brown eyes, saw sincerity and certainty.

Then he smiled, a smile that tugged at her heartstrings. 'It's quite simple really.' He took a deep breath. 'I love you Amara. I love you and I wanted you to know. I understand how much the idea of love scares you. I understand what a risk it is. And I understand that there's a good chance that you don't love me back. There's no reason why you should. But if there is any chance any possibility that I can win your love then I will do my hardest to try.'

Amara realised her whole body was shaking, her heart so full it could burst and she realised she had to say something, had to tell him her truth. And as the butterflies soared and flapped with disbelief, she allowed happiness to surge and she smiled at him.

'You stole my lines,' she said on a gulp and a hiccup as tears of sheer joy threatened.

Confusion touched his eyes and then his face broke into an answering smile.

'Because I love you. That's what I wanted to tell you, why I asked to meet. I love you and yes, it is terrifying, but it's also exhilarating and wonderful. And I missed you so much these past days, so much it hurts. And yes, I will probably always be scared of losing you, but I am far more scared of walking away from you. And being with you is worth the risk, you are worth any risk. I want to be with you, by your side.'

'And I want to be with you. I want to wake up beside you, I want to hold you, I want to love you and walk by your side for the rest of our days.' He reached into his pocket. 'Amara Rossi. Will you marry me. For real. A true marriage, a true fairy tale, a true happy ever after, together.'

'Yes, I will. With all my heart.'

He took the ring from his pocket, the same beautiful ring that glittered and glinted in the afternoon sun that slanted in from the windows and slipped it onto her finger. 'A perfect fit,' he said and she smiled at him.

'Just like us.'

He took her hands in his. 'And for the record, this marriage is strictly and solely for love.' His smile widened. 'So much love. I can't believe this is really happening, that it's true. That you love me.'

'Believe it.' Amara gave a soft laugh, held her hand out to show him the ring. 'It's you and me. Forever.'

'Forever,' he echoed.

Amara hesitated. 'But if our marriage helps

with the board that would be fine with me. It wouldn't devalue our love in anyway.'

'I appreciate that, but I worked out another way.'

'What?' She moved round so now she was next to him on his side of the booth and it felt like coming home, sent further waves of happiness floating through her. 'How? What happened with your father, with the board?' Amara asked.

'I brokered a deal,' Gio said. 'I decided to stop being a chess piece. To stop trying to prove I am a real Romano. I contacted my brothers.'

Amara reached out, took his hand. 'That must have been difficult.'

'Only Antonio agreed to see me, but we did meet and…' Gio shrugged. 'And we'll see. I think, I think there is a chance, a real chance, we may forge some sort of relationship. Max… is still set against me and as for my father I don't think anything can change how he feels about me. But when we met, Antonio did admit he doesn't agree with what my father is doing. That he has tried to speak with him but to no avail.'

'So what did you do next?'

'I called a meeting. In my boardroom.' Gio gave a small smile. 'My territory. The company that I am proud of, passionate about. My grandparents were there and my father and brothers.

And I confronted my father, called his bluff. I told him he could try to prove my grandmother lacks capacity but he would fail. I showed him letters from two top consultants. I told him he could keep the shares he has but he isn't getting any more. That my grandparents are hanging onto those. That I won't join the board. But the articles would be changed and then my brothers can join the board, be part of the decision-making, that after a while they would be given some shares, as well. But that my grandparents would retain control, and I would act as their proxy and if need be, I would be brought on board in the future. If everyone couldn't work together.' He squeezed her hand. 'Once I stopped worrying about being a real Romano everything became clear. You helped me see that, Amara. Helped me see that I am a good person in my own right. That I have nothing to prove to anyone. That Romano Confectionery isn't my holy grail. You changed me.'

'And you changed me. You switched on a switch I thought was locked shut. You showed me how to live, how to see life through a different filter. To see that solitude is safe, but there is so much more to life than safety. That I am more than just an heir to the Rossi estate. I have other skills and talents. Other ideas. You showed me that it is right to welcome Lorenzo and Daisy to the family, but that I need to do it out of more than a moral duty, that I need to do it with an open heart and mind. You have shown me that I am capable of letting people in, letting people close.' She blinked back tears. 'I love you, Gio.'

'And I love you, Amara.'

She reached out and poured them both a glass of the ruby-red wine. 'To us,' she said.

'To us,' he repeated.

She grinned at him. 'And I have food to go with it. The owner and chef here is a family friend and he has made us some amazing things. All fairy tale themed. There is something he has called The Glass Slipper, which is made of crystallised ginger and oh, so many ingredients, and he's made a Let's Change the Pumpkin and a Magic Wand. I can tell you all about them.'

'And I will love listening to every word. But first I bought you a present.' He reached down and handed her a bag.

She opened it and now her smile lit her face. Inside was a snow globe, a fairy tale castle nestled against a backdrop of mountains and as she shook it and watched the swirl of flakes, she knew that fate had brought them to this perfect precious moment, the start of their happy ever after.

# EPILOGUE

AMARA LOOKED AROUND the living room at Alavario castle and felt her heart sing with joy and a near disbelief at how much life had changed in a few months. Knew it was all thanks to a chance encounter in the Bavarian Alps, brought about by so many random events, so many dominoes falling in different times and places, culminating in a mistake made by a hotel staff member, that had left one table for two single diners.

Gio and Amara, Amara and Gio. Yet as she looked across at Gio now, Amara knew with all her being that they were meant to be together, that if they hadn't met at that table then they would have met somewhere else. Somehow their paths would have crossed because they were meant to be.

And now here they were celebrating their engagement with family. That idea too was incredible. Filled her with happiness as she took a moment to watch the assembled guests. Aurelio and Ava were stood together and the protective way Aurelio stood by his wife, the obvious love between them brought a tear to her eye.

The past months had wrought such a change in their relationship with Gio, a change that Amara knew had made Gio happy, had laid some demons to rest. The older Romanos had stood by their apology for excluding Gio, had done all they could to remedy past wrongs. And Gio's surprise, Gio's happiness had made Amara happy, made her able to give Aurelio and Ava a chance. And as she had got to know them, to like them, she'd begun to see just how complex relationships could be. That people weren't black and white, that Gio was right. People could do something wrong, something inexcusable, but it didn't define the whole of them.

The same went for Antonio; Gio had been right to say that he thought there was potential there and again Amara felt admiration surge for the man she loved, for his capacity to forgive, his capacity to see good in people. And so slowly tentatively the half-brothers were forging a relationship. Enough so that Antonio had accepted the invitation to attend this family gathering, was stood chatting to Gio and Vittorio as she watched all three men laugh. And as Vittorio placed an affectionate hand on Gio's shoulder, Amara felt the familiar sense of happiness that the two men she loved so much had clicked, got on so well, so easily. Gio turned his head now and caught her eye and her heart swelled with a love that she knew he could see in her eyes, just like she could see the love in his.

But now as her gaze continued to sweep the room, she took in Lorenzo, her half-brother and for a moment she watched him, saw that he too was watching the group, and she wondered how it made him feel. She knew that Vittorio and Gio had both tried to engage with Lorenzo, suspected that her half-brother was standing aloof through his own choice.

In the past months, Lorenzo had visited the estate only the once. The initial planned meeting, once so dreaded by Amara, had been part revelation and part surprise. Seeing him had impacted both herself and Vittorio, because he was the spitting image of Roberto. Amara's dad, Lorenzo's dad. Their dad. Now as she studied him, of course she could see some differences, but overall the hair, the aquiline jut of his nose, the unexpectedly dark blue of his eyes was true Rossi.

But looks apart, Lorenzo had been at pains to state that he expected nothing from the Rossis. Any idea Amara had had of being displaced had been well and truly erased. He'd said he simply wanted to meet them out of curiosity, but he accepted he had no claim.

The rest of the meeting had been a little awkward though Lorenzo had been perfectly civil, had been respectful and courteous to both Vittorio and Amara and had even agreed to return with his sister at some point. A point that hadn't materialised.

Amara took a deep breath, suddenly aware of how this tableau must feel to Lorenzo. All these people. All this family. Talking and laughing, at ease with each other. Yet he was stood looking on. Not that he looked uncomfortable, or distressed. He looked… As though he was perfectly content to observe.

But Amara felt a curiosity and more than that, she wanted to include him. They were related and she knew how much it would mean to her grandfather if Lorenzo chose to became family.

She headed towards him and saw him tense slightly, though his smile was perfectly civil.

'I just wanted to thank you for coming.'

He nodded acknowledgement. 'It was kind of you to ask me.'

Yet she sensed the words were ambiguous and had some hidden meaning. ‘We wanted you to be here. After all, we are family,’ she said.

‘Technically speaking,’ he said, then shook his head. ‘I apologise. That was rude. I simply meant to make it clear that Daisy and I know we have no claim on you.’

‘I understand that and it goes both ways. We know we have no claim on you.’ She knew that her grandfather had contacted Lorenzo a couple of times but had been scrupulous to exert no pressure, had told Amara and Gio he was simply keeping the door open. ‘We know it must have been a massive shock to find out the truth. But I wish Daisy could have come today. We would very much like to meet her when or if she wants to.’ She hesitated. ‘So no pressure, but I wanted you to know that truly we would welcome you.’

He looked at her and as she met those dark blue eyes, Amara was hit by a punch of emotion, because somehow just for an instant she could see an echo of Luca in Lorenzo’s eyes. Like her twin’s—a slightly mischievous look, but also a look that seemed to read her.

‘You sure?’ her half-brother asked. ‘After all, it must have been a shock to you, as well. I wouldn’t blame you for feeling resentment.’

A penny dropped. 'Is that why Daisy hasn't come today? Is that why you haven't been back? Because you think I don't want you here?' She could hardly blame him if he did.

'That's not the only reason, but we would understand if you'd rather we faded into the background, disappeared into the woodwork.'

Amara took a deep breath. 'I wouldn't. We wouldn't. Of course we feel a moral obligation to acknowledge the link, but I promise it is more than that. I want to welcome you into the family. I would like you and Daisy to become part of the family in the ways that count. Not just because we share a father but because we like each other.'

'Maybe we won't like each other,' he said, his words only half light.

'Then so be it.' After all, Amara was pretty sure that Max and Salvatore would never become part of their family circle. And she was good with that. 'But I'd like to try. If you want to?'

There was a pause as Lorenzo considered her words. 'I'll talk to Daisy,' he said in the end. 'Maybe next time we'll come together.'

Amara smiled. It wasn't a promise—it was tenuous—but she hoped it was a start.

'And of course I really hope you'll both come to our wedding.' She grinned at him, hoped to introduce a less emotional topic. 'Though it won't be as grand as Prince Ashan's, which I saw that you will be attending.' She'd been reading a lot of bridal magazines of late and had seen an article about the forthcoming nuptials of Prince Ashan, prince of a small but prosperous island principality in Indonesia. And in that article had been mention of Lorenzo, who was to be the prince's best man. Amara had stored the information away, hoped it would be a good conversational topic.

But now as she saw Lorenzo's expression she saw she'd thought wrong. For an instant she'd been sure she recognised a hint of panic in those blue eyes, the expression once again reminiscent of her brother when he was anticipating trouble. Then it was gone and Lorenzo's expression shuttered, his lips slightly set, his jaw set. But all he said was, 'Yes, I will be. I'm looking forward to it.'

But somehow Amara sensed that wasn't the case at all and it was with relief she saw Gio approach. A relief she sensed her half-brother shared.

She smiled up at Gio, 'I was just telling Lorenzo how glad we are he came today.' Not exactly true, they had just been discussing a royal wedding, but somehow she was sure Lorenzo appreciated her dropping that topic.

'Absolutely.' Gio nodded. 'In fact, whilst you're here I'd like to pick your brains. I read recently that you've floated your company on the stock exchange.'

Amara smiled as the conversation turned to business, knew Gio was doing his best to put Lorenzo completely at ease. Hoped anew that this truly was the start of a relationship.

Because now the idea of being a part of a family filled her with joy. She would never forget Luca or her parents or her grandmother, would always grieve them, but it would no longer stop her from living, from risking, from protecting herself from joy and closeness. To all the people in this room right now. And she hoped to one day include Daisy as well and perhaps one day children of her own would join in here.

An image of their children running round the room, playing hide-and-seek in the castle. Gio throwing them up in the air, family outings. Pictures of a true fairy tale coming to life. Her and Gio's happy ever after.

* * * * *

*Look out for the next story in the*
*Long-Lost Rossi Siblings trilogy*
*Coming soon!*

*And if you enjoyed this story, check out these other great reads from Nina Milne*

Secret Royal's Napoli Reunion
Their Mauritius Wedding Ruse
Cinderella's Moroccan Midnight Kiss

*All available now!*